Bond of Destiny

Also From Larissa Ione

~ DEMONICA/LORDS OF DELIVERANCE SERIES ~
Pleasure Unbound (Book 1)
Desire Unchained (Book 2)
Passion Unleashed (Book 3)
Ecstasy Unveiled (Book 4)
Eternity Embraced ebook (Book 4.5) (NOVELLA)
Sin Undone August (Book 5)
Eternal Rider (Book 6)
Supernatural Anthology (Book 6.5) (NOVELLA)
Immortal Rider (Book 7)
Lethal Rider (Book 8)
Rogue Rider (Book 9)
Reaver (Book 10)
Azagoth (Book 11)
Revenant (Book 12)
Hades (Book 13)
Base Instincts (Book 13.5)
Z (Book 14)
Razr (Book 15)
Hawkyn (Book 16)
Her Guardian Angel (Book 17)
Dining With Angels (Book 17.5)
Cipher (Book 18)
Reaper (Book 19)
Bond of Destiny (Book 19.5)

~ MOONBOUND CLAN VAMPIRES SERIES ~
Bound By Night (book 1)
Chained By Night (book 2)
Blood Red Kiss Anthology (book 2.5)

~CONTEMPORARY/WOMEN'S FICTION ~
Snowbound
The Escape Club (Summer 2022)

Bond of Destiny

A Demonica Novella

By Larissa Ione

1001 DARK NIGHTS
PRESS

Bond of Destiny
A Demonica Novella
By Larissa Ione

1001 Dark Nights

ISBN: 978-1-951812-53-9

Published by 1001 Dark Nights Press, an imprint of Evil Eye Concepts, Incorporated

Sign up for the 1001 Dark Nights Newsletter
and be entered to win a Tiffany Key necklace.

There's a contest every month!

Go to www.1001DarkNights.com to subscribe.

As a bonus, all subscribers can download FIVE FREE exclusive books!

Dedication

For Stacey Tardif. A whole dedication, just for you. :) Love you, girl!

Acknowledgments from the Author

I want to send out huge thanks to everyone on the Evil Eye/1001 Dark Nights team, especially Liz Berry, M.J. Rose, and Jillian Stein for their continued and amazing support and enthusiasm. And not just for me, but for all their authors. What an incredible company you have built. You keep reaching new heights, and I truly believe there is no limit to where you can go. Love you ladies so much!

And Kim Guidroz, holy crap, girl, I know I tell you this a lot, but I am so grateful for all your hard work. I put you through a lot of last-minute changes, and you haven't killed me yet. Kind of makes you a saint, and I love you for it!

Judie Bouldry, oh, man, you have been through a lot recently, and somehow, you're still there for me. I'm so happy to have you with me all these years after THE Kindle Cover! Here's to many more years! Love you!

And finally, I want to thank all the incredible members of my Larissa Ione's Underworld group on Facebook. I don't get to play there as often as I'd like, especially lately, but you have kept it an energetic, fun respite during a crazy time. Kat Furgerson Daugherty and Cheryl Johnson, you ladies are life savers, and I can't even begin to tell you how glad I am to have you at the helm. You are pretty damned awesome.

One Thousand and One Dark Nights

Once upon a time, in the future…

I was a student fascinated with stories and learning. I studied philosophy, poetry, history, the occult, and the art and science of love and magic. I had a vast library at my father's home and collected thousands of volumes of fantastic tales.

I learned all about ancient races and bygone times. About myths and legends and dreams of all people through the millennium. And the more I read the stronger my imagination grew until I discovered that I was able to travel into the stories... to actually become part of them.

I wish I could say that I listened to my teacher and respected my gift, as I ought to have. If I had, I would not be telling you this tale now.
But I was foolhardy and confused, showing off with bravery.

One afternoon, curious about the myth of the Arabian Nights, I traveled back to ancient Persia to see for myself if it was true that every day Shahryar (Persian: شهريار, "king") married a new virgin, and then sent yesterday's wife to be beheaded. It was written and I had read that by the time he met Scheherazade, the vizier's daughter, he'd killed one thousand women.

Something went wrong with my efforts. I arrived in the midst of the story and somehow exchanged places with Scheherazade – a phenomena that had never occurred before and that still to this day, I cannot explain.

Now I am trapped in that ancient past. I have taken on Scheherazade's life and the only way I can protect myself and stay alive is to do what she did to protect herself and stay alive.

Every night the King calls for me and listens as I spin tales. And when the evening ends and dawn breaks, I stop at a point that leaves him breathless and yearning for more. And so the King spares my life for one more day, so that he might hear the rest of my dark tale.

As soon as I finish a story... I begin a new one... like the one that you, dear reader, have before you now.

Glossary

Aegis, The—Society of human warriors dedicated to protecting the world from evil.

Fallen Angel—Believed to be evil by most humans, fallen angels can be grouped into two categories: True Fallen and Unfallen. Unfallen angels have been cast from Heaven and are earthbound, living a life in which they are neither truly good nor truly evil. In this state, they can, rarely, earn their way back into Heaven. Or they can choose to enter Sheoul, the demon realm, in order to complete their fall and become True Fallens, taking their places as demons at Satan's side.

Harrowgate—Vertical portals, invisible to humans, which demons use to travel between locations on Earth and Sheoul. Very few beings own, or can summon, their own personal Harrowgates.

Pricolici—Werewolves who are born as such. Can only conceive during the breeding heat unless medically altered, and offspring are almost always born werewolves, even if the father is Vârcolac. See: Vârcolac.

S'genesis—Final maturation cycle for Seminus demons. Occurs around one hundred years of age. A post-*s'genesis* male is capable of procreation and possesses the ability to shapeshift into the male of any demon species.

Sheoul—Demon realm. Located on its own plane deep in the bowels of the Earth, accessible to most only by Harrowgates and hellmouths.

Sheoul-gra—A holding tank for demon souls. A realm that exists independently of Sheoul, it is overseen by Azagoth, also known as the Grim Reaper. Within Sheoul-gra is the Inner Sanctum, where demon souls go to be kept in torturous limbo until they can be reborn.

Sheoulic—Universal demon language spoken by all, although many species also speak their own language.

Vârcolac—Werewolves who were once human, turned into wargs by the bite of another. Both born and turned werewolves can infect a human with lycanthropy. Offspring conceived during the breeding heat are occasionally infected with lycanthropy in the womb and are born as werewolves.

Warg—Name by which werewolves often call themselves.

Watchers—Individuals assigned to keep an eye on the Four Horsemen. As part of the agreement forged during the original negotiations between angels and demons that led to Ares, Reseph, Limos, and Thanatos being cursed to spearhead the apocalypse, one Watcher is an angel, the other is a fallen angel. Neither Watcher may directly assist any Horseman's efforts to either start or stop Armageddon, but they can lend a hand behind the scenes. Doing so, however, may have them walking a fine line that, to cross, could prove worse than fatal.

Chapter 1

Stacey Markham knew she shouldn't be driving in a snowstorm. It was dumb. Beyond dumb. Yes, the late April storm had come in faster and harder than expected, and yes, she was in her four-wheel drive Jeep with studded snow tires. But right now, what she really needed was a snowmobile.

"Dammit, Dad," she muttered as she fought to keep from sliding into a ditch on the curvy mountain road. He'd insisted on going out to stock up on supplies, and he wouldn't listen when she told him not to. The only way she'd gotten her parents to stay home was to take them the supplies herself. "You'd think after fifty years of living in the mountains of Colorado, you'd know better."

A gust of wind caught her SUV, sending it into a spin on the icy road. White snow and the Jeep's red hood filled her vision, blurred into a swirled peppermint candy by the breakneck speed. When the vehicle finally came to rest, backward in the middle of the road, she gasped in relief. On one side of the road was a sheer rock cliff. On the other, a treacherous drop into a partially frozen river. She sat there for a moment, letting her heart rate settle into a steady rhythm instead of the erratic spasms that made her head pound.

She gripped the steering wheel to stop her hands from trembling and eased the Jeep back into the right lane. Visibility was near zero now, so limited she wasn't sure where, exactly, she was. She should be within a couple miles of Jillian's driveway, and if worse came to worst, she could probably shelter there. Her best friend was currently staying at her Greek residence, but her caretaker would definitely be home.

Caretaker.

It was a fancy and wholly inaccurate word for what he was.

Putting the ruggedly handsome man, who happened to be a werewolf, out of her mind, Stacey concentrated on driving at a snail's pace down the mountain. She couldn't see the pavement, could barely see the front end of her Jeep.

This was stupid.

So stupid.

She cursed her life choices, beginning with her former career as a sheriff's deputy and ending at this very moment. Dying in a blizzard when it could have been prevented was going to suck. She should have taken the job at the Demonic Activity Response Team's Honolulu office when they offered it to her two years ago. Instead she'd opted to remain in her small Colorado hometown as the sole DART agent, in charge of dealing with the occasional demon incursion.

She could be lounging on a warm beach right now, soaking up the sun and drinking piña coladas. Instead, she was going to freeze to death in a snowstorm or burn to death in a fiery crash.

Somehow she made it a mile in under fifteen minutes without ending up in a pile of flaming metal at the bottom of a ravine. Her hands were cramped from gripping the steering wheel so tightly that it'd probably have permanent finger dents, and her jaw hurt from clenching it.

At this rate, it was going to take her hours to get back to town—

She screamed as the back end of her Jeep fishtailed hard and caught the shoulder. The next few seconds were a spinning blur of terror and ice and snow, followed by confusion and pain.

The first things that became clear as the confusion faded, was that her rig had flipped onto its side and the cloying odor of gas burned her nostrils. She couldn't hear the engine running, but the ringing in her ears could have been drowning it out. The next thing she became aware of was pain in her head. And arms. And left leg.

Oh, and she was lying on the crumpled driver door, her left shoulder resting in snow and broken glass.

Shit.

Her hand shook as she fumbled around to unfasten her seatbelt. Took a dozen tries from the awkward position, but she finally managed to free herself. Darkness made things even worse, and when she felt the vehicle shift and slide, panic sent her into a desperate scramble to escape the cab.

Agony screamed up her leg and hip as she squirmed her way upward, reaching for the passenger door. She gave silent thanks when she discovered that the window had broken out of it, eliminating the need to fight with the heavy door while trying to extricate herself.

As quickly as she could and fueled by fear, she heaved her battered body out of the window and onto the door of the Jeep. Instantly, stinging snow and wind scoured her exposed skin. Thankfully she had on her parka, but her gloves were still somewhere in the truck, and there was no way she was climbing back inside to find them.

The Jeep shifted again, slipping a few inches, spurring her into action. She leaped from the SUV just as it slid down the incline, this time for several feet before catching on what appeared to be a tree trunk or a boulder and flipping upside down, crushing the cab she'd just been inside.

Holy hell. I could have been inside that.

Shaken by her close call, Stacey trembled so violently she could barely use her hands to scale the ravine. It took her far longer than it should have, and by the time she reached the road, her fingers were numb, her arms felt like wet noodles, and her legs could barely hold her upright.

Before she could even take two dozen steps, her stomach rebelled, and she lost her late lunch of a steak burrito and refried beans from the new Mexican place in town. When she finally stopped retching, she started down the mountain, struggling in the fresh snow.

Best guess, about six inches of snow had fallen on top of the foot and a half that had yet to melt after a record snow winter, but the wind had created deep drifts that were already making the road impassable. She cursed herself over and over for attempting the drive even though she'd known better than to try.

Now she was too far from town to walk, but Jillian's driveway was ahead. Somewhere. She wasn't sure exactly where, but she did know Jillian's property was the closest occupied residence. All the other buildings out here were vacation homes or hunting cabins. And while Stacey could break into one and take shelter if needed, committing a crime was going to be a last resort.

The wind shrieked like a Frost Howler, a demon she'd encountered during her DART training with the head honcho, Kynan Morgan.

They were cold. Cold like this blizzard.

Shivering violently, she limped through the darkness, looking for Jillian's mailbox. Surely it wasn't far now. It had to be close. Had to be.

And with a little luck, she wouldn't freeze to death before she found it.

* * * *

The thing Tracker loved most about heavy snow was the silence that came with it. Right now the wind was howling, but once it died down, the forest would fall into the kind of peace one had to experience to understand.

Peace was something he'd neither experienced, nor understood, until recently, when his slave bond was transferred to Jillian Cardiff, a human who'd been given no choice in the matter. He wished he could feel bad about the fact that they were now linked for life against her will, but it was the best thing that had ever happened to him.

Before this, his nearly seventy years of life had been defined by misery and fear, never knowing from one minute to the next if he was going to be beaten, tortured, or killed. He'd spent the majority of his existence believing that the only peace he'd ever get would be when he died.

And even then it was questionable.

He knew too well what happened when you lost your life within the confines of Hell. The soul was immortal, and demons were skilled at making a person wish that wasn't the case.

Tonight, though, as he stood on his cabin porch peering into the darkness, the silence was broken by the feeling that something…wasn't right. He inhaled deeply, letting his werewolf-enhanced sense of smell try to identify that something.

Then he saw it. Motion on the driveway.

His gaze narrowed and focused, homing in on a two-legged figure trudging up the driveway against the wind and drifts of snow. His hackles went up, and a growl rattled his chest.

You're my favorite guard dog. Good boy. Good Whine.

Reseph had taught Tracker about the Box of Bad Shit, the place where you shove all the bad memories when they pop up at inconvenient times to fuck with your life. Like now.

Tracker stuffed that shit in his BOBS, locking down the memory of his old name and his second master, second of many. Jillian had returned his birth name to him, and the old demon bastard wasn't around to beat him anymore anyway.

Stealthily, he eased off the porch and into the shadows cast by the light streaming through his cabin windows. The snow stung his bare feet, but the cold didn't affect him as much as it affected humans. A werewolf, or warg, as his people called themselves, from birth, he was stronger, faster, and tougher than his homo sapien counterparts. Even in human form, his hearing was better, his sense of smell far superior, and his eyesight was at least twice as sharp.

And now that awesome eyesight locked onto the person struggling through the snow as Tracker moved as quickly as he could toward Jillian's cabin. The figure in the driveway was almost there. A female figure, he thought. Human? Probably. Harmless? Likely. But he wasn't taking any chances.

Whoever it was, they weren't getting inside his master's home.

He approached from behind, the wind shifting as he got within forty yards, and he finally caught the stranger's scent.

Definitely female. And definitely not a stranger.

"Stacey!" he called out, but the wind swallowed her name almost before it fell from his lips.

She kept going, swaying with the force of the gale, and then she went down, disappearing in a deep drift.

Shit. Jillian would never forgive him if her friend froze to death in a storm, mere feet from the front door.

In the past, failure on such a scale would have earned him unending agony for weeks, maybe months. Potentially, even death.

But neither Jillian, nor her mate, Reseph, had ever harmed him. Heck, with the exception of the day he'd arrived on her farm, called by the bond that had been transferred to her, neither had so much as used a harsh tone or said a cross word to him. Jillian, especially, had treated him with nothing but kindness and respect.

Still, instinct and over half a century of living in fear as a slave overpowered logic, and it took a precious few seconds to break free of the invisible chains that rendered him unable to move.

A gust of icy wind finally knocked some sense into him, and he loped through the snow to where he'd seen Stacey go down. At first, he didn't see her. In the few moments since she'd fallen, snow had covered her, and if not for a bit of the gray fur ruff around her parka's hood fluttering above the layer of white, he might have lost a lot of valuable time searching for her.

She didn't move as he gathered her in his arms and hauled her back to his cabin. He wasted no time in taking her to his bedroom and placed her limp body on the mattress. She moaned as he removed her coat and boots, but before he went further, he stoked the fire in the wood stove and cranked up the heat.

Now what? He couldn't get her to a hospital by car, but if he could rig a sled, maybe he could take the snowmobile to the nearest Harrowgate. He immediately dismissed the idea as insane. In this storm he'd get them both killed.

But Jillian could send Reseph. As one of the Four Horsemen of the Apocalypse, the warrior known to many as Pestilence, Reseph could summon his own gates, allowing him to travel from point A to point B in an instant. He could get Stacey to safety.

Tracker fetched his phone from the kitchen counter, but after three failed attempts to make a call, he finally realized cell service was out. Hopefully the power would hold—

The lights flickered. Once. Twice.

Everything went dark.

Fucking perfect.

The log walls creaked under the force of the storm as he peeled Stacey out of her cold, wet clothes, leaving her only in teal underwear and a matching bra. Her skin bore the marks of past injuries, long, narrow blemishes on her torso, a puckered scar on her shoulder, and a mass of scar tissue on her leg. He wondered what had happened to her, but that was a question for later. Right now her skin was like ice, pale and mottled, and she had multiple cuts, abrasions, and bruises on her left side.

He had no medical training and no experience with cold weather injuries, but he did know that her blue lips and fingers weren't a good sign and that she needed more warmth than blankets alone would provide.

By the faint light cast by the fire in the living room, he towel dried her ice-crusted dark blonde hair. She'd lightened it since the last time he'd seen her. He liked it.

When her hair was as dry as possible, he used the towel to wipe her face before stripping down to his own underwear—black boxer briefs he'd gotten on a shopping trip with Reseph.

Sad that Tracker hadn't known how to shop when he'd first arrived. Hell, he hadn't even worn underwear. None of his masters had ever provided him with them. The garments had been weird at first, but Reseph had insisted that boxer briefs were the best and that "chicks dig them."

Tracker hadn't known what that meant, either. Chicks? Like, baby birds? And why would they "dig them?"

There'd been so much to learn.

He slipped beneath the covers and eased up to Stacey. He sucked air when his abs touched her freezing back, and he outright shivered as his legs pressed into the backs of her thighs. Damn, she was cold. He could feel it seeping into his muscles, all the way to the bone.

As he wrapped his arms around her, he shuddered. "You'll be fine, human. I swear it."

She had to be. Jillian was the kindest person he'd ever known, but if her best friend died on his watch, she just might kill him.

Chapter 2

Stacey was freezing. Not the kind of freezing where you got goosebumps and shivered until you put on a coat or came inside from out of the snow. No, this was a marrow-deep freeze that made muscles feel like slabs of meat in a butcher's cold storage locker. Warmth surrounded her, but it didn't reach her insides.

Like deep fried ice cream.

Which sounded amazing even through the brain fog that left her unsure where she was.

Somewhere dark. Was she in her bed? Her mind raced as she struggled toward coherence. She'd gone to see her parents… Was she in their spare bedroom?

Almost immediately, she dismissed that idea because she remembered trying to drive home. In a snowstorm.

Oh, that's right. She'd been a freaking idiot. And she'd paid for it when her Jeep had spun out on the slippery road and tumbled down a ravine.

She remembered climbing out of it and making her way through the blizzard. Remembered finally reaching Jillian's driveway. Remembered thinking she was going to freeze to death.

So she probably wasn't in *her* bed.

Squinting in the darkness, she tried to make sense of what was going on, but her surroundings were pitch black. There was definitely a mattress under her and blankets on top of her, so she was in *someone's* bed. Outside, the storm was still raging, screaming through trees and shaking the building.

Inside, someone was breathing right behind her.

Her frozen heart got an injection of adrenaline and a sudden jump-start.

Arms. There were arms around her. And a big, hard, warm body against her back. And…and…was that…an *erection* pressing into her butt?

Oh, God.

"It's okay." A deep, gravelly voice drifted to her ears, and she nearly screamed. Would have, if her breath hadn't been lodged in her throat. "It's me. Tracker."

Relief that she wasn't in some psychopath's bed was tempered by the realization of being in bed with the guy she'd been secretly lusting after for years but had been too afraid to approach. Well, not afraid, exactly. Intimidated, really. And, okay, maybe a little afraid. He *was* a six-and-a-half foot tall werewolf, after all.

Plus, Jillian said he was off limits. Maybe not necessarily in those words, but she'd caught Stacey drooling over Tracker once, and there had been a note of both disapproval and caution in the way Jillian had said that Tracker had had a rough life. Which was probably putting things mildly.

No one who had been owned by demons for decades could possibly escape unscathed.

Jillian hadn't gone into great detail about his past, and Stacey didn't know if the reason was that Jillian simply didn't know all of it, or if she was respecting Tracker's privacy, or if it was too awful to talk about.

In any case, Stacey had limited her interest to admiring him from afar and fantasizing about him in the confines of her own bed.

And oh, what fantasies they were…

"Stacey." Tracker's gruff voice made her shiver. Or maybe it was the fact that she was ice cold. He must have felt it, because his strong arms tightened around her. "You're in my cabin. Power's out."

That explained why it was dark. "What time is it?"

He lifted his arm, and suddenly the insanely bright glow of his watch cast enough light to see what appeared to be a small bedroom. A rustic dresser sat against the log walls next to a curtained window.

"A little after two A.M."

Which also explained the darkness.

"Go back to sleep," he murmured. "I've got you."

His words lulled her into a sense of safety and comfort, and the next thing she knew light was streaming through cracks in the curtains.

Tracker was no longer in bed with her, and the delightful aroma of coffee and breakfast sausage drifted into the room.

Yawning, she sat up and immediately regretted it. Her head pounded, and every muscle screamed like it was stretched beyond its limit. She looked down at herself—in nothing but her bra and underwear—and winced at the bruises that mottled her skin. She'd definitely taken a beating in the wreck.

"There are clothes on the dresser for you," Tracker called out. "And power is back on."

"How did you know I was awake?" she called out, wincing with every word.

When she asked exactly that, his answer was simply, "I'm a werewolf."

As if that explained everything.

Well, it kinda did. One of her DART training handbooks—volume three of twenty—was entirely about shapeshifters, and it had an extensive section dedicated to were-creatures. Enhanced hearing in human form seemed to be common in all varieties of weres, but especially were*wolves.* And to get even more specific, werewolves who were born that way instead of turned into one via a bite had the best hearing of all. They had the best of everything, in fact.

She stood stiffly, biting back a groan as she shuffled over to the dresser where she found a black pair of what must be Tracker's sweatpants, a giant forest green Eddie Bauer sweatshirt, and thick socks. She had to cinch the pants tight around her waist, and the shirt swallowed her down to midthigh, but at least she was warm and cozy even if she looked like a child trying on her dad's clothes.

When she reached for the socks, she knocked something off the dresser. She picked it up, a nickel-sized silver disk with what appeared to be angel wings on one side and a crown of birds on the other. She'd have to take a closer look later.

When her feet weren't freezing on the cold wood floor.

She slipped on the socks and followed her nose into the open concept living room-slash-kitchen. Tracker was scrambling eggs on the stove, his big body dwarfing the appliance. With every motion, muscles rippled beneath his white T-shirt. She'd seen him countless times working outside in the sun, shirtless and bronzed, and she knew exactly how toned and hard he was under the thin cotton material. Although, come to think of it, she'd never seen him in shorts, but she'd bet that beneath those well-worn jeans that fit like a glove, his legs would be pure muscle.

He'd also cut his gorgeous, sandy hair since the last time she'd seen him. He'd gone from Chris Hemsworth in the second *Thor* movie to Chris Hemsworth in the third one. So he was still as hot as ever. Maybe even more so.

Definitely more so.

"Your boots are drying by the front door," he said, his gaze fixed on the cast-iron frying pan. "Your clothes are in bad shape, but I put them in the washer to see if some of the blood will come out. Not sure your coat is salvageable, though. The arms are ripped to shreds."

She cursed. Her Fjällräven parka had cost a fortune, and her favorite pair of jeans couldn't be replaced. They could only be mourned. So comfy and perfectly broken in, not to mention that they'd outlasted several boyfriends.

"I can always borrow some of Jillian's clothes."

"Cell service is out." He scooped the eggs onto a platter and turned to her. "I can't contact her for permission."

"She won't mind. We've been borrowing each other's stuff since high school." His inscrutable, dark gaze said that she hadn't reassured him. "It's okay. Really."

"She entrusted me to watch her house and property."

"Yes, but—"

"She's my master." His voice cracked like a whip, the sharp echo lingering as he dropped more sausage links into the pan. "I can't go against her wishes."

Stacey cringed. She freaking hated the "master" bullshit, and she knew Jillian did too. But no matter how many times Jillian had told him to call her by her given name, he refused to do so directly. For the longest time, not even an explicit order could make him call her anything but "master," or "mistress." Recently, she'd made inroads with "ma'am," and there might be a few other honorifics he used, but he'd never once called her Jillian to her face. Only when talking to others.

"You don't have to go against her wishes," she argued. "I know where her spare key is, so I can go get what I need."

The smell of burning sausage filled the air, but Tracker ignored it, his body taut, his lips pursed in thought. He was probably trying to figure out if part of his duties included physically stopping his master's best friend from entering her house.

"Don't worry," she said, not wanting to stress him out further. "I don't need anything right now."

That seemed to placate him, and he turned back to the stove, leaving her to take her first real look around the cozy cabin.

Sparsely furnished, with just a rustic brown leather couch, a coffee table, and a newer, sixty-inch flat screen TV on a stand, his cabin was clean and tidy. He could use some art on the walls, though. Jillian had let him pick out the furnishings, but he hadn't chosen any decorations…or anything aside from the bare necessities. It had actually been Reseph who made Tracker get the TV to help him learn about the human world and keep him entertained.

She peeked down the staircase that Jillian said led to his "bark box," where he sometimes locked himself up on nights of the full moon.

"Besides," she said, "I should be able to go home soon."

He snorted as he flipped the sizzling sausage links. "Define soon."

"Tomorrow?"

This time he flat-out laughed, and it occurred to her that it might be the first time she'd ever heard him do that.

Stacey shuffled, all stiff muscles and aching joints, to the front window where she swept aside the heavy green insulated curtains. She should have been able to see the barn to the left, Jillian's cabin to the right, and the black Tacoma pickup she'd bought for Tracker to use in the driveway.

But nope, there was nothing but hard-packed snow against the panes of glass, all the way to the top.

"Oh, wow. That's one hell of a drift."

He gestured to the front door with his sausage tongs. "You're gonna love that."

Uh-oh. She carefully opened the heavy oak door and stared at the wall of white. There was maybe an inch of space to spare at the top. Maybe.

"Holy crap." A few clumps fell and broke apart at her feet, and she kicked them aside as she closed the door. "I've never seen this much snow, and I've lived here all my life."

"I like it." Tracker transferred the links to a plate already piled high with sausages. "We didn't have snow anywhere I lived before."

"Really?" she asked, and then mentally kicked her own ass for asking that. Of course he didn't have snow. He'd lived in Sheoul, better known as Hell to humans, his entire life. There was even that whole saying about Hell freezing over. "Oh, never mind. I suppose there's not much snow in Sheoul."

"There's a lot of snow in some regions." Tracker dumped a package of hash browns into the pan. "But I never lived in one."

"Oh. Huh. Learn something new every day, I guess." That info was probably in one of the DART training manuals she hadn't gotten to yet.

Every joint screamed at her as she dragged her sorry ass to the kitchen and swept back the curtains on the dining room window. The drifts weren't bad on this side of the house, but the heavy snow completely obscured Jillian's cabin, just forty yards away.

"How much snow do you think we got so far?"

"A foot and a half, maybe." Tracker piled the food onto a big platter. There must have been at least a dozen eggs, two dozen sausages, and a serious mountain of potatoes. How much did he think she ate? How much did *he* eat?

"Last I saw, just before cell service went out, they were saying we'd get another foot. It's a record storm."

Yeah, she wasn't getting out of here for days. She might not find her Jeep anytime soon, either, which would be an insurance nightmare. Hopefully cell service would be back up soon so she could call her parents. They were going to be worried sick.

Tracker placed the platter and a couple of forks and plates on the two-person table. "Are you hungry?"

A moment ago, she'd have said no. But with the tantalizing aroma of savory meat and peppery potatoes in the air, her stomach growled like a beast out of Hell.

And she knew what a lot of them sounded like.

"I'm starving."

His amber eyes narrowed into slits as he watched her, so she tried not to limp. If the way his lip twitched into a smirk was any indication, he knew.

"As soon as the phones are working again, I'll call Jillian. Reseph can get you to a doctor," he said, confirming her suspicions.

And hell, no. Jillian might be comfortable leaping through the magic portals her husband created out of thin air, but Stacey wasn't. She still wasn't over the fact that he had turned super evil and nearly ended the world.

Nope. She wasn't getting into his Magical Mystical Murder Portal. Not ever.

"I'll be fine." She pulled the dining room chair out from the table. "I've had worse than a sprained ankle before." Some aspirin would be great, though.

Tracker set a steaming mug next to her plate, and she inhaled, getting a morning fantasy aroma-fest of savory food, coffee, and masculine, outdoorsy male. It was what breakfast in bed should smell like.

Her hormones got all jittery because damn, he smelled better than breakfast. She'd blame her reaction on a savior complex, but the truth was that he always got her heart racing.

"How much worse?" he asked. "I saw some of your scars last night."

Her cheeks grew warm at the reminder that he'd seen her practically naked. And he'd been pressed up against her like that, his erection nestled along the curve of her lower spine. She reached past him for the coffee, wishing it was a toddy instead. She could use something stronger for this conversation.

"Well," she said, "I broke my leg skiing when I was in high school. And I got shot in the arm once. Just a graze when my cousin did something stupid." She shrugged and spooned some eggs and potatoes onto her plate. "When I was a kid, I separated my shoulder in a fall from a horse. Last year I needed stitches after a demon raked my rib cage with its claws." She plunked a couple of sausages onto the eggs. "I'm sure there are more examples, but I'm going to shove my face full of food now."

A smile flirted on his lips, and it struck her that it was the first time she'd seen anything even remotely resembling a smile from him. But then, as a slave, he probably didn't have much to smile about.

Disgusted by his situation and the fact that neither she nor Jillian could do anything about it, she did her best to put it out of her mind as she dug in before he even took his seat.

"Thank you," she said, after she'd swallowed a bite of scrambled eggs. "For breakfast and for last night."

"You were lucky I found you." The chair creaked as it absorbed what was probably two hundred and fifty pounds of solid werewolf. "What happened? Why were you out in the storm?"

She took a sip of her coffee. She'd prefer it iced—and laced with Baileys—but she wasn't going to complain. "I wrecked my Jeep coming down the mountain from my parents' house. And yes, I know I shouldn't have been out in the storm in the first place."

He cocked one tawny eyebrow. "It *was* stupid."

Hmph. He might be the hottest thing she'd ever seen, but he was still annoying. "How do you know it wasn't an emergency?"

"Was it?" He glanced over at her as he loaded his plate with most of the remaining food on the platter.

"No," she mumbled. "Trust me, I'm kicking myself. How did you find me, anyway?"

He swallowed a bite of sausage. "I sensed you."

"Sensed me?" She paused with her forkful of eggs halfway to her mouth. "How?"

There was a moment of silence as he peppered his potatoes. "I felt that something wasn't right."

"Is that a werewolf thing?"

"Maybe. Could be a slave bond thing too." He shrugged. "I don't know much about werewolves."

"But…you're a werewolf."

"Yes." His eyes remained fixed on his plate, and she realized he rarely met her gaze. He never really had before today, but she'd assumed it was because whenever she'd been here, it had been to visit Jillian, and he'd been busy elsewhere. Now it was just…odd.

"You were born a werewolf, right?" According to her handy-dandy DART training manuals, there were major differences between *Pricolici*, or born werewolves, and *Vârcolac*, who were turned into werewolves. Differences that went beyond their physical abilities, all the way to their behavior, mating habits, and lifestyles. They also didn't like each other much. There had been actual wars between the two types. Kynan had mentioned that they were still engaged in what was essentially a cold war.

"Yes." Still talking to his food.

"Then why don't you know much about them?" She took a bite of burned sausage, which was actually the way she liked them. She'd always liked her meats cooked extra well done.

Tracker's voice went low, almost to a whisper. "I was sold into slavery within an hour of birth."

The food in her mouth turned to dust. "I didn't realize," she swallowed dryly. "I'm so sorry."

He said nothing, and they sat there in awkward silence as they ate. Well, he ate. She mostly picked at the rest of her meal. She wanted to talk to him, had so many questions, but he wasn't exactly the easiest person to chat with. And he definitely didn't seem like he wanted to converse.

So she gave him space as he cleaned up his plate and then took it to the sink. "I can make more if you're still hungry."

"I'm fine, thank you." She pushed away from the table. "I'll wash the dishes. It's the least I can do."

Shaking his head, he reached for the skillet. "It's my duty."

"No." She laid her hand on his forearm and stopped him. "You cooked, so I'll clean."

"But I'm a—"

"I said no." Her voice was harsher than she'd intended, but dammit, he needed to understand that his purpose was not to serve. Not her, not Jillian. Not anyone. Not anymore. "You saved my life, Tracker. I owe you, and even if I didn't, it's what people do. They share the work, and I'm sure you have other things to do."

For the longest time he didn't move, and she wondered if she'd gone too far. Offended him, maybe. Just as she was about to ask, he gave a curt nod and stepped aside.

"Thank you." He might have given in, but his body language, the way he glanced around and shifted his weight, said he was uncomfortable with the situation. "I'm going to dig us out. Will you be okay for a couple of hours?"

"Of course, but do you really have to go out in this storm?"

The floor creaked under his weight as he moved toward the back door, where his snow boots sat on a mat near the coat rack. "I need to check on the animals."

Oh, right. She still wasn't sure exactly why Jillian continued to keep some of her rescued animals now that she and Reseph were spending most of their time in their other residences. Before they'd moved, Stacey had volunteered to take some of them, but after she'd gotten the job with DART it became clear she wouldn't have the time required to give them the kind of care they needed. So Jillian had sent most of her critters to sanctuaries in Colorado—along with generous donations to keep them, and the rest of the sanctuary animals, in luxurious comfort. But some, like the two inseparable goats and the twin miniature donkey brothers, had remained.

"Well, I don't know how much help I can be, but I can—"

"No." He shoved his feet into his boots. "You need to rest."

"But—"

He swung around, a glow of feral determination in his eyes. "Cleaning up after breakfast is one thing, but my mistress would not be happy with me if I allowed you to do physical labor while you're injured."

"Jillian doesn't—" She cut herself off before she said it. Before she said, *Jillian doesn't own you.* Because the fact was, Jillian did own him. And it made Stacey sick. It wasn't Jillian's fault, and nothing could be done about it. But dammit, it was just so…horrible. "Jillian doesn't need to know."

Tracker shrugged into his parka. "I will not keep anything from her."

"I'm curious," Stacey said. "Is it because she's your…master?"

He appeared to consider his answer as he tugged on his gloves. "With any of my other masters, the answer would have been yes. But my mistress doesn't need the slave bond to hold my loyalty."

"Were your other masters that bad?"

The pain in his expression said it all. He didn't need to say anything. And he didn't. He flipped up his coat hood, opened the door, and disappeared into the wall of wind and white.

Chapter 3

Tracker spent an hour shoveling snow, and that hour only got him halfway to the barn. The snowblower would have been a big help, except that it was inside said barn. So was the tractor with the snowplow blade.

He should have prepared for the storm better. He could only be thankful Jillian wasn't here to see his lack of preparation. Bad enough that Stacey was here to see it.

Stacey.

His heart skipped a beat at the mere thought of her. He might not know what to think about her, but his body had its opinions.

She'd been around a lot before Jillian and Reseph moved, so he'd seen her, of course. But other than a few words of greeting now and then, they'd never actually talked.

He'd watched her, though. At first, it had been out of caution. He was suspicious of everyone who came near Jillian. She was his number one priority, and when Reseph wasn't around to protect her, Tracker was.

But eventually he'd come to realize that Stacey wasn't a threat, and if anything, the female was a capable warrior. And he knew that not because she used to be a sheriff's deputy and was now an agent with DART, but because, like himself, she'd spent time with Reseph training with a bow and arrow, sparring, and practicing shooting.

He'd seen her in action, and it was impressive.

For a human, anyway.

And, for a human, she was what Reseph would call "hot." Not that Reseph had said that about Stacey. It was what he said about Jillian, and whenever he said it, the heat in his pale blue eyes left no doubt about what it meant.

Stacey, in Tracker's opinion, was also hot. So, yeah, when he'd first started watching her during her visits, it was out of caution. Then it was because she made his blood heat, and that was something that had never happened to him before.

Yes, he'd been aroused, but in the past it had been because it was a natural response to whatever situation his masters had exposed him to—or forced him into.

Demons were big on orgies.

But this was different. When he looked at Stacey, he saw a female who was toned but still rocking curves made to cushion a male's powerful thrusts. And he liked that she didn't wear a lot of makeup, leaving her creamy skin supple and smooth, which he'd discovered last night when he'd stripped her down.

He'd done his best to be respectful and not lust after a freezing female, but now that she was back to normal, he couldn't stop thinking about how her skin would taste under the caress of his tongue. He already knew how it felt against the length of his body.

And he wanted more.

Growling at the futility of the direction of his thoughts, he dumped another shovelful of heavy, wet snow alongside the pathway and looked back at the work he'd done in the last few minutes. There was already another couple of inches behind him.

Fuck.

Not that he minded the work. It was basically all he had to do. His job was to take care of Jillian's property, the house, and the animals. That was all. Even if he spent the next month doing nothing but shoveling snow from her two hundred acres all day long, it would still be the easiest month of his entire life.

And that was the problem. At least, that was what was eating at him right this minute.

As he shoveled, he couldn't get Stacey's question out of his mind.

Were your other masters that bad?

Yes, yes they were.

He tried not to think about them. Thanks to advice from Reseph and a lot of self-discipline, he'd managed to put his previous owners out of his thoughts for years. For the most part, anyway. He'd had no reason to dwell on them, not since Jillian had given him a new lease on life.

She'd given him kindness. Freedom. Respect. Things he'd never had before.

For months after he'd come to live here, he hadn't been able to believe his luck. Surely, it was too good to be true. Every time she or Reseph spoke to him, he'd flinch inside, afraid that after the kindness would come pain. Because that was what he'd learned about kindness. It was always followed by horrific agony, either because the "kindness" had actually been cruelty designed to lull him into feeling something other than misery, or the person delivering the kindness had regretted it and followed up with punishment.

When he was eight years old, one of his masters gave him a sweet pastry, a rare treat, and after Tracker ate it, his master whipped him until he vomited it up.

Just for amusement.

So Tracker had learned to fear and distrust anything even remotely nice.

But gradually he'd discovered that Jillian was truly decent and had no hidden agenda. She was a good person who treated him like an equal, which terrified him on a different, and unexpected, level.

Equality simply wasn't allowed. He was a slave, bonded to whatever master was currently holding the leash—a leash that still, technically, belonged to the Neethul Slaver Guild. If the slavers, who he'd always known as *malibites,* ever learned that she was decent to him…he wasn't sure what they'd do, but it wouldn't be pleasant. For her or him.

He could handle it. But he couldn't deal with the thought that she might suffer. His only consolation was knowing that whoever harmed even a hair on Jillian's head would face the wrath of her mate, a male who had nearly broken the world and who would take pleasure in destroying everyone who had been even remotely involved in hurting her.

So, yeah, she'd earned Tracker's loyalty the way no one ever had. Not his former masters. Not the family who had sold him into slavery. Not even Harvester, the angel who had transferred his bond to Jillian. Because while he was grateful that Harvester had given him to the best master he could ever hope for, she had also been cruel to him. Less so than others, but still.

Cursing the direction of his thoughts, he shoveled with renewed determination, putting his angry energy into every heavy scoop.

And damn, this shit was deep. His biceps were burning by the time he made it to the barn, and he groaned when he saw the five-foot deep drift piled high against the door. He could enter through the big double doors on the other, less exposed side, but he'd have to dig a trail, which would take another hour.

Definitely not worth it.

Fifteen minutes later, he finally got inside the building. The air smelled of straw and hay mingled with the scent of the animals, who greeted him with excited snorts and bleats.

The power was back, but it wasn't needed. The *brimidium* stone on the pedestal near the center created a soft yellow glow that kept the barn both warm and lit.

The goats, two brown pygmy Nubians, stood up on their hind legs to watch him over the top of their stall, and the miniature donkeys rushed their stall door.

"You guys hungry?"

They were probably stir-crazy as well as hungry, but he couldn't put them out in this weather. He supposed he could let them out of their stalls so they could run around the barn, though. He'd have to clean up their messes later, but that wasn't a big deal. Poor things needed to stretch their legs, and he could clean their stalls while they were wreaking havoc in the barn.

He fed them first, and while they scarfed their food he cleaned and refilled their water buckets. He contemplated getting out the snowblower and clearing the area around the barn, Jillian's house, and his own cabin even though it was still coming down hard. If he didn't do it, the snow was going to be so deep that even the snowblower was going to have a hell of a time getting through it.

Decision made, he gassed up the machine and moved it near the door just as it opened. Snow and cold air blasted inside with Stacey. She was still wearing the clothes he'd given her, but she'd gotten her shredded jacket out of the dryer.

With the fur-lined hood around her face, her cheeks pink from the cold, she looked adorable. Which annoyed him. He really didn't need to be thinking about her in any way that wasn't strictly related to *she's my master's best friend. Untouchable. Off limits.*

"You were supposed to stay inside," he said gruffly.

"I wanted to say hi to the critters. I haven't seen them in a while." She missed a step when she looked over at the pedestal holding the stone. "Is that rock...glowing? And emanating heat?"

"Yes."

Warily, she drifted closer. "What is it?"

It's a *brimidium* stone. I got it in Sheoul."

"Whoa." She took a hasty step back. "It's a stone from Hell? Are you serious? Jillian let you bring that thing inside her barn?"

"It's harmless."

Harmless, yes, but Jillian had been furious that he'd entered Sheoul, and it was one of the few things she'd forbidden him to do again.

"Are you sure it's not cursed or powered by evil or something?"

"It's powered by the Earth," he said as he bent to tighten the snowblower's gas cap, "but the stone itself can only be obtained in Sheoul."

She walked around it, eyeing it suspiciously and keeping at a distance. "Then why aren't they sold here in the human realm? Those things would solve a lot of energy problems."

"And there's your answer."

She stopped pacing long enough to glance over at him. "You're saying that there are humans who are aware of their existence but don't want to cause damage to the energy industry?"

"That's what Reseph says." He shrugged because he didn't care about any of it. What did the Horseman call it? First world problems? "But the stones are extremely rare. I don't think they're much threat to any power company."

"Interesting." She scratched one of the donkeys behind its ear. "If they're so rare, how did you find one?"

"One of my former masters owned a mine. I knew where to find them."

"Oh. That's good, I guess."

He supposed it was good that he had access to the stones, but otherwise there had been nothing good about his former master. The demon had forced Tracker to hurt mine workers who didn't perform well enough, but Stacey didn't need to know that. Humans, he'd discovered, were kind of squeamish.

"And he didn't mind you taking one of his precious stones?"

"Hagfrun is dead, so no." Hagfrun's death at the end of a Silas demon's blade had resulted in Tracker's bond being transferred to the Silas demon, who had been even worse than Hagfrun. Fortunately, the Silas's life had been cut short by a necromancer who had been marginally less awful as a master.

"Someday," Stacey said, "I'd like to know more about your life."

Tracker laughed bitterly. "I don't think you would."

And he didn't want to share anyway. He'd even avoided telling Jillian much. He didn't like talking about it, and he definitely didn't want to be looked at differently. Because that was another thing he'd learned about humans. They judged people harshly based on their pasts.

And, as he'd learned from his pack members, werewolves did too.

"Well, not right now." She looked around the barn, her gaze landing on the pitchfork leaning against the bales of hay. "How can I help? I'm pretty good at mucking stalls."

She was determined to get him in trouble with Jillian, wasn't she? He admired her persistence. Heck, he admired a lot about her, from her skills with weapons, to her loyalty to her friends. He'd seen how she'd been skeptical about Reseph, her determination to protect Jillian worn right on her sleeve. But she was also willing to change her mind as she got to know the Horseman, and now they seemed to get along well.

So, yeah, he admired her. A lot.

Not that his admiration could go anywhere. Even if she weren't Jillian's best friend, slaves weren't allowed to mate. They couldn't even date. And sex? That could only be had at the discretion—or command—of his master.

Jillian had told him that he was free to do anything he wanted—except enter Sheoul—and he supposed that meant sex too. But even if Stacey wanted him in that way, and it was okay with his master, he had no idea how to make it happen. And definitely not while she was injured.

Still, he allowed himself a lingering look, remembering how she'd felt tucked up against him in bed this morning. Her body had finally warmed up and her skin had been soft, her generous curves smooth, and he'd been inappropriately stirred with every little move she'd made.

"Tracker?" she prompted again. "What can I do to help?"

"You can go get warm in the house while I finish clearing snow around the barn."

"Why not wait until after the snow stops?"

"I want to take down the drifts to make it easier to plow later."

"Fine," she said, sounding disappointed. "But I *will* help clear snow after the storm is over. I've lived through thirty Colorado winters, so it's not like I can't handle a shovel or snowblower."

He had a feeling arguing would be pointless. And if she wanted to operate the snowblower on the paths, he could use the plow to clear the driveway and bigger areas.

"Okay," he muttered. "But later."

Taking her victory with a smile and a sexy strut, Stacey went back to the house while he got to work clearing the area around the barn and the path between the barn and his cabin and Jillian's. It took longer than expected now that the temps had gone up and the new snow was extra wet and heavy, and by the time he was done, he was in desperate need of a shower.

The goats, Rick and Evie, named after the main characters from *The Mummy*, one of Jillian's favorite movies, bleated at him as he put away the snowblower. But the donkey brothers, Sam and Dean, seemed restless, braying as they ran in circles around the barn.

"What is it, boys?" he asked, but even before he finished speaking, the hair on the back of his neck stood up and an uneasy feeling filtered through him. Something…something was off.

It was a shimmer of wrongness on his skin that he couldn't identify, but it was there.

Carefully, he eased over to the windows, but he didn't see anything suspicious, and by the time he opened the barn door, the sensation had dissipated.

So far, the storm had brought record snow and a human female to his doorstep.

He wasn't sure he even wanted to know what else it might have brought.

Chapter 4

While Tracker was outside clearing snow, Stacey figured she'd do something useful, especially since the power was back. Maybe she'd cook something for him. She'd done enough snow clearing in her life to know that when he came in from outside, he'd be simultaneously hot *and* freezing, and definitely starving.

She pawed through his cupboards, but sheesh, he didn't have much in there besides cans of soup, chili, hash, and Spam. His spices were only the most basic—garlic, onion, and chili powders, salt, pepper, and oregano, but her frugal mom had taught her to cook with what you had, so she could work with it. And she did manage to find some spaghetti pasta and a jar of sauce, so that might have to do.

Just as she reached for the fridge handle, Tracker's cell phone rang. Awesome. Service was working again. She glanced over and saw Jillian's name pop up. Should she answer?

Yeah. She should.

"Hey, Jillian!"

"Stacey?" Jillian's stunned voice sounded tinny. "Is that you? I meant to call Tracker. Did I accidentally call you?"

"This is Tracker's phone. He's outside right now. Hope it's okay that I answered."

"Yeah, yeah, it's fine. But I'm confused. Where are you?"

"Long story." She sank down on the couch. "I'm at his cabin. I kind of got stuck here because of a blizzard."

"That's why I was calling. I heard about the storm and wanted to make sure he was okay. You too, but you haven't been answering your phone. I couldn't get through to Tracker either until just now."

"Cell service has been down," Stacey said as she threw her feet up on the coffee table. "And I don't have my phone with me."

"Why? What's going on? How did you get stuck there?"

"Don't freak out, but—"

"*But what?* Oh, my God, Stace, what happened?"

"I got into a car accident—don't worry," she added hastily, "I'm fine. But it was during the blizzard, and Tracker found me. He brought me back to his place, and now I'm trapped here until the roads are cleared."

"That could be days. Holy shit. As soon as Reseph gets back from Australia, I'll have him gate you home."

Eh…that was a hard pass. "What's going on in Australia?" Stacey got up to fetch her cup of coffee on the kitchen counter, her stiff joints groaning with every step.

"Ugh. Long story." Jillian blew out a breath. "You know how Azagoth destroyed Sheoul-gra and released billions of demon souls into the world?"

Yeah, she knew. Everyone knew. Humans included. It was, literally, a disaster of Biblical proportions. Sheoul-gra had been the place all demon souls went after death. Evil human souls, too. Then, one day, the being known by many as the Grim Reaper had freaked out and destroyed the realm, and millions, maybe billions, of those souls were released. And not just released. They'd taken corporeal form and were now causing trouble in both Hell and the human realm.

It seemed that demons and evil humans were obsessed with revenge. Who knew.

Besides everyone with a brain, anyway.

"Have those newly released demons moved to Australia or something?"

It seemed like Australia was always getting shit on.

"They're trying. Australia has been evacuated of humans, and good demons are trying to develop a country of their own, but evil demons are trying to get rid of them."

Not long ago, Stacey wouldn't have been able to draw a distinction between evil demons and "good" demons. But since Jillian's marriage and Stacey's own experience in DART, she'd come to understand that not all underworlders were bad. Tracker, for example, was a werewolf, but he wasn't evil. He didn't even go crazy and kill people on the nights of the full moon. Maybe that was because he locked himself up, but still.

The fact that he did lock himself up rather than hunt humans was pretty much proof that he wasn't evil.

"So what is Reseph doing there? Are the other Horsemen with him?"

"Thanatos and Ares are. They're drawn to the death and war. So far, there hasn't been any starvation to draw Limos."

"But there's plague, I guess?" Reseph, as the Horseman known as Pestilence, was drawn to plagues and pestilence against his will and would leave Jillian for horrific scenes in both the human and demon realms for days, even weeks or months.

"Apparently, it's how some of the evil demons are trying to get rid of the others. Do you know who Eidolon and his sister Sin are?"

Who didn't? Eidolon was only the most respected demon doctor in the world. He even ran his own hospital, Underworld General. And his sister was famous for her existence as the only female of their sex demon species.

"I've never met them, but they work with DART a lot, so I know who they are." Plus, her big boss, Kynan, was Eidolon's brother-in-law.

And Sin was responsible for breaking Reseph's Seal and turning him into Pestilence. So, yeah. She knew who the two Seminus demons were.

"Well," Jillian said, "Sin is some sort of infectious disease expert, so she and Eidolon are working to get the plague under control. I hear they're making progress—yay—so Reseph should be home soon."

Stacey sank down on the couch again, being careful not to spill her coffee. "We're living in some strange times, aren't we?"

"You can say that again." Jillian sighed. "Are you sure you're okay?"

"A little bruised, but I'll survive."

There was a pause. "How's Tracker?"

"He's fine too." Something about her friend's hesitation flipped Stacey's suspicious switch. It was something her old boss at the sheriff's department said was "unusually well developed." Her gut had gotten them into, and out of, a lot of sticky situations. "Why do you ask?"

"I don't know." Jillian took a sip of something. She'd been hardcore into English breakfast tea with cream lately, so that was Stacey's guess. "He's just...he's hard to read, you know?"

That was the understatement of the day.

"I worry about him," Jillian continued. "And he's not good with people, so with you there..."

With me here? Stacey set down her mug on the coffee table. "You think I'm, what, harming him in some way?"

"Oh, God, no. Not that. If anything, company is probably good for him. I think the only socialization he gets is when he goes into town for animal feed or groceries."

Socialization. Like what people did with dogs.

Stacey knew Jillian didn't mean it that way, though, and feeling silly for getting defensive, Stacey relaxed. "Is that why you didn't give up the goats and donkeys?"

"Yeah." Jillian sounded a little embarrassed. "He needs something to do, and I didn't want him getting too involved with his pack."

Stacey frowned. "I thought his pack gave him up as a baby."

"They did. Assholes," Jillian growled. "But werewolves are drawn home by the full moon, and some of his masters used to let him go for runs with his pack now and then. Mental health breaks or some shit. Like they cared about his mental health."

Jillian had never really shared much about Tracker's past, so this was all news. "So he knows the members of his pack? His family? Parents?"

"He does, but it's hard to get him to talk about them. It's hard to get him to talk about anything."

"Huh, I hadn't noticed." She tucked a pillow behind her aching back. "So why are you concerned about his pack?"

"Besides the fact that they sold him into slavery?" Jillian's bitterness practically dripped from her words.

"Well, yeah. Besides that."

"I don't know." Jillian took another sip of her mystery drink. "Some of the things he's said makes it sound like they're not very nice to him. I actually thought about asking Reseph to go have a chat with them. But I don't think Tracker sees them often, and I worried it might only make things worse anyway. You know, like a parent getting their kid's bully in trouble at school."

Stacey could definitely relate to that. In high school she'd had a standing feud with Gina Perini, head cheerleader and mean girl extraordinaire. One day, when Gina and her bitch squad trapped her in the bathroom and shoved her head under the water faucet, her parents had freaked out. Stacey begged them not to go to the principal, but they hadn't listened.

Her life for the rest of the school year had been pure hell. Gina had gotten all her friends involved in bullying her. If not for Jillian, it would have been even worse. But Jillian had a knack for showing up at exactly the right time, and finally, in their senior year, Gina and her friend Vickie made the wrong move beneath the bleachers at a football game.

Stacey and Jillian had made a damned good team, and Gina had to cheer the rest of the game with a black eye, while Vickie slunk home minus most of her hair extensions.

Which Stacey and Jillian had used to decorate Gina and Vickie's lockers the following Monday.

No one ever messed with Stacey again.

Since then, Gina moved away, but as a deputy Stacey had gone to Vickie's trailer three times for domestic abuse calls. It was a sad situation with a methhead boyfriend, and she hoped Vickie had finally gotten out of it.

The front door creaked open. "Oh, hey, Tracker just came in," Stacey said. "Do you want to talk to him?"

"No, it's okay…wait. Yes."

"Okay, hold on." She started toward Tracker as he shrugged out of his snow-covered parka. "Oh, and before you go, is it okay if I break into your house to borrow some clothes? And maybe some stuff to cook with? Tracker's pantry is pretty pathetic."

"Do whatever you need to do." Jillian paused. "Is he eating okay?"

"As far as I can tell." Stacey lowered her voice, although doing so was probably futile, given Tracker's supernatural hearing abilities. "I just think he doesn't cook much for himself."

Jillian sighed. "I had Suzanne come over and teach him how to cook with human ingredients, but I don't think he gets much practice."

"Suzanne?" For some reason, jealousy reared its ugly head at the thought of some other woman teaching Tracker anything.

"Yeah, Suzanne. Remember? She's got that popular cooking channel on YouTube?"

"Oh, right. Azagoth's daughter." Stacey couldn't believe how casually she'd said that. Like, no big deal that the Grim Reaper's daughter was a famous chef who had popped over to Stacey's best friend's house to teach her slave how to cook.

Man, Stacey's world was weird now. But was it even weirder that she liked it? Liked being "in the know" about stuff that most humans only speculated about?

"Okay, here's Tracker." She handed him the phone and left him alone while she went to clean the kitchen.

After he hung up, she turned to him. "Did Jillian tell you it's okay if I go raid her house?"

Tracker didn't look at her as he kicked off his boots. "She says I'm to allow you access to anything you want."

"Including you?" she asked, teasing, but he stiffened and bowed his head.

"I assume so," he said, his voice tight, dark, and Stacey instantly regretted her ill-timed humor.

"Oh, damn, Tracker. I didn't mean it like that. I would never take advantage of my friendship with you or Jillian to make you do anything. I swear."

He shrugged and started toward the bedroom. He still wasn't looking at her. "I'm used to it."

Her heart…it just broke. Spilled sorrow like blood into her chest cavity. She wanted to kill everyone who had ever hurt him. Who had ever made him feel so powerless and used.

"I would never. I promise." She reached out and gently placed her hand on his forearm, and he finally glanced her way. "Look, I joke around a lot, and sometimes my jokes fall flat. People don't always get me. Trust me, I've looked like a fool on many occasions."

"I like jokes. There weren't any before. Not ones that were funny." His tawny brows slammed down. "And I don't think you're a fool. And anyone who thinks that *is* a fool."

Heat flooded her cheeks, and she hurried to change the subject. She wasn't comfortable with compliments. She never had been. Her mom used to say that if a man complimented you, he wanted "nasty things," and if a woman complimented you, it meant she was jealous.

Stacey didn't believe either was always true, but she'd still grown up not learning how to take compliments well.

So she changed the subject.

"So, um, Jillian said Suzanne helped you learn to cook."

"She did." He gestured to the magazine stand next to the couch, which appeared to hold a handful of books. "She gave me some cookbooks, but they didn't help much."

"Why not?"

"I was taught to read in Sheoulic, not English. Jillian and Reseph taught me the basics, but…" He looked down at his stockinged feet. "I can't read many of the recipes."

"Well, then," she said, fetching one of Suzanne's cookbooks. "I guess we have something to do while we're holed up. Why don't you take a hot shower and change into some dry clothes, and then let's make something."

Stacey got the impression that Tracker didn't show joy very often. And he didn't now. But that little golden glint in his eyes was the equivalent of a grin from anyone else.

She wished her phone wasn't at the bottom of a ravine because she really, really wanted to text Jillian right now.

Company is definitely good for him.

And I'm company.

* * * *

Tracker showered while Stacey raided Jillian's pantry for ingredients needed for something called spaghetti carbonara.

He was actually looking forward to learning how to cook something new. He'd been eating mostly stuff that came in cans for a long time. Thanks to Suzanne, when he needed a break from canned meals, he could cook some basics like pancakes and macaroni and cheese, or dishes that translated from Sheoul, like scrambled eggs and sausage.

And sure, the sausage here in the human realm was made from different things, and the eggs came from chickens instead of carnivorous dire hens, but they cooked up the same. Tasted better, though. So far, everything in the human realm tasted better.

A lot better.

Every once in a while Harvester would bring home fast food burgers and fries, a special treat he'd savored while dreading his next meal of whatever underworld feast her Ramreel chef prepared.

Human food was the best.

Now he wondered what, exactly, had gone into Sheoulic hamburger and sausage.

As he dried himself, he heard the back door open and close.

Stacey's voice called out, breathlessly, and for some reason, that gave him a warm sensation in his groin. "Honey, I'm home!"

Honey?

Baffled, he wrapped the towel around his hips and stepped out of the bathroom as Stacey was kicking off her shoes, her hands clutching several full plastic grocery bags.

"Honey is bee sugar." He knew because Harvester had kept it around to sweeten her hot drinks. It also gave angels a boost of emergency energy. "What you said makes no sense."

She laughed. He was learning to love that sound. It echoed around his cabin and made it feel less empty.

"Honey is also something people call other people. 'Honey, I'm home,' is kind of a…joke."

"Oh. Okay." He liked that she joked around with him, even if he didn't understand. Her jokes weren't cruel, and that was all he needed to know.

Still standing on the welcome mat in socks, her gaze dropped to his bare chest. She tracked a renegade drop of water as it went lower, past his navel, winding between the swells of the muscles in his abs, and the heat in his groin went wood stove hot.

"Wow, that's…a good look on you."

She kept saying stuff he didn't understand. "It's just a towel. Why would you say that?"

"I get the feeling you haven't been complimented a lot. It's something people should do more, you know?" She lugged the bags to the kitchen. "No matter what my mom says."

He wasn't sure how to respond, but the warmth in his groin spread, flowing upward through his veins and into his chest. Her words felt good.

She looked back and gave him another once-over that made shivery goosebumps erupt on his skin, and then she placed the near-bursting plastic bags on the counter.

"I hope you don't mind, but I used your phone to call my parents to check on them and let them know I'm okay."

"You can use it whenever you want."

"Thank you. As soon as you're dressed, we can get cooking. I mean, unless you want to do it in just that towel. I won't complain." Her wink told him it was another joke, and this time he grinned because, if he wasn't mistaken, she was flirting. And despite the fact that she was basically forbidden fruit, he liked it.

No one had ever flirted with him before.

He couldn't wait for the cooking lesson, wasted no time in throwing on a pair of jeans and a burgundy Colorado Avalanche sweatshirt. The shirt was one of his favorites, a gift from Reseph, who sometimes got together with his brother Ares to watch hockey games.

When he came out of the bedroom, Stacey was done unpacking the bags and was staring at the jars, cans, other food items, and utensils on the counter.

"The good news," she said, "is that Jillian had the major ingredients we need for a couple of different recipes. The bad news is that we'll have to improvise on a few things. Oh, and there's no electricity in her cabin."

"Is the water still running?"

She nodded. "Houses here are built for extreme temperatures, and it's not that cold right now."

Still, he checked the weather app on his phone. The outside temps were hovering around twenty-eight degrees, and Jillian had once said that she didn't worry about the pipes until the temperatures plunged into the negatives for an extended period of time. But that was with heat in the house. Right now there was none of that.

"Maybe I should start a fire in her wood stove."

Stacey paused as she loaded his cupboards with stuff from the bags. "I don't think it's necessary, but if you want to do that, I'll get everything together for our cooking lesson."

Leaving Stacey to put away supplies, he hurried over to Jillian's house and got a fire going. The trouble was, he wasn't comfortable leaving a fire unattended overnight. He'd either have to stay on Jillian's couch or let the fire go out tonight.

Either way, he'd be sleeping on a couch, though. Stacey could have his bed for as long as she was stuck here.

The thought gave him a *holy shit* realization, that he would be okay with her being stuck here.

Seriously. Holy shit.

He was a loner, happiest when there was no one around. Being alone meant no one was going to force him to do anything. No one was going to hurt him. He'd even been secretly glad when Jillian and Reseph moved away, because for the first time in his life, he'd been under no pressure.

And yet, he was enjoying Stacey's company, and he couldn't wait to get back to his cabin.

Upon his return, she smiled at him from where she was mixing something in the blender she'd brought over from Jillian's.

"Want a margarita?"

"What's a margarita?" He'd heard of them, but he wasn't sure what they were.

"It's a magical beverage made with tequila and lime-based mix that will go well with our meal." She winked at him. "Don't ever let anyone tell you that Italian food and margaritas don't go together."

He wasn't sure why they wouldn't go together, but he nodded anyway and watched as she poured the light green slushy mixture into two tall glasses. She handed one to him and held hers out.

"Cheers."

He'd seen this ritual before. On TV. They were supposed to clink their glasses together. He had no idea why, but what the hell.

"Cheers."

She watched him with curious, sparkling gray eyes as he took a drink. Huh. It was pretty tasty. Burned a little, but he could get used to it.

"You like?"

"I…like."

"Excellent. You have good taste." She clinked her glass against his again. "So now we'll get to cooking." She led him to the open cookbook and pointed at the recipe. "Do you know this word?"

He frowned. "No."

"Do you understand the measurements?"

Nodding, he dragged his fingertip along the list of ingredients. "Suzanne taught me about cups and teaspoons."

"Okay, good. So we need one cup of Parmesan cheese…"

Chapter 5

Tracker decided he loved to cook.

When Suzanne had been here to teach him, he'd been so nervous about screwing up that he hadn't enjoyed it. It wasn't that she hadn't been a great teacher. In fact, aside from Jillian, she was the friendliest person he'd ever met. She'd been patient, kind, and generous. But he hadn't been Jillian's slave for long, and he'd still been paranoid. In his old life, if he'd used too much or too little salt, he could be whipped. If he dropped a spoon, he could be deprived of food for days.

So, no, learning something new had been a serious endeavor and nothing to smile about.

But Stacey made it fun. Well, Stacey *and* the margarita. He'd never been allowed to have alcohol before, and he was beginning to understand why. It made him feel. No, that wasn't entirely accurate. It *allowed* him to feel.

And right now, as he shook the jar of Parmesan cheese over the bowl of pasta, he felt pride. And when he looked over at Stacey, her lips curved into a smile, he felt a lot more than that.

He…wanted.

It was a dangerous thing to feel, but the euphoria tingling through him didn't care. Stacey called it a "buzz." He wondered how long it would last. And if he could have more margarita slush.

He looked down at the tangle of pasta and inhaled the savory scent of garlic and bacon. "Can we make something else tomorrow?"

"You got it." She took a sip of her margarita, and when she licked the salt off the rim with the tip of her pink tongue, his mouth went so dry he had to take a gulp of his own drink. "Of course, until we can get to a store, we're pretty limited by what we have available between Jillian's place and yours. But we'll figure something out."

He grinned, and it struck him that he'd never been happier than he was at this moment.

It was so unexpected, so foreign, that it almost felt wrong.

"Tracker?" Stacey touched his hand, and his heart did an alarming fluttery thing. "What's the matter? You look confused."

"I think…I think it's the buzz."

"What is?"

How did he explain it? His thoughts weren't as sharp as they should be, and he wasn't sure if all of it could be because of the alcohol. "I feel strange."

"Strange how?"

Did he dare say it? "Happy," he said tentatively. And when Stacey's smile slid off her face, he backtracked. "I'm sorry. Is that wrong? Did I—"

"No! Tracker, no." She squeezed his hand, but it might as well have been his heart. Compassion wasn't something he'd experienced much of before. "It's just that it makes me sad that your life has been so hard. No one deserves what you've gone through." Abruptly, she brightened and gave him a blinding smile. "But let's not think about that right now. We have this delicious dinner to eat."

Agreed. His mouth was watering as he carried the bowl to the table while she turned on the TV. "Aren't we eating over here?" he asked.

"I thought some ambience would be nice."

He pretended to understand as she turned on a music channel, soft instrumental sounds.

"My mom likes to say that music aids in digestion," she continued.

"Is it true?"

"I have no idea, but it's nice, don't you think?"

One of his masters used to dine to the screams of his prisoners. This was way better. "It is."

Before she sat, she fetched the pitcher of margaritas and poured a little more in each of their glasses.

"I like that stuff," he said, reaching for his.

She laughed. "Well, be careful. It's dangerous."

He froze with the glass halfway to his mouth. "Dangerous, how?"

"It'll get you into trouble, let me tell you. I once had too many and woke up in the back of a stranger's car." She gave him a pointed look. "I do not recommend." A dribble of icy liquid dripped down the side of her glass, and she mopped it up with a napkin as she continued. "Obviously, you don't have to worry about that. But you should still go easy, especially if you're not much of a drinker."

"Drinker?"

"Of alcoholic drinks."

"I've never had one before today."

Her brows shot up. "Oh, then you *definitely* should take it easy."

Keeping her warning in mind, he pushed the glass away and loaded his fork with pasta. Anticipation made his mouth water as he took a bite.

Flavor exploded on his tongue. Salty, peppery, creamy… It was the best thing he'd ever eaten. The food he'd cooked with Suzanne had been good, but he'd been too stressed to really enjoy it.

Not so this time. This time he was relaxed, and the female sitting with him wasn't mated. Even better, she wasn't the Grim Reaper's daughter. Suzanne's mate must have balls made of brimstone.

It made him wonder about Stacey's father.

"You said you wrecked your car on your way home from your parents' house." He glanced over at her as she twirled noodles around the tines of her fork. "What are they like? Do you have any brothers or sisters?"

"I have one brother. He moves around a lot with his job. He's in Florida right now." She stopped twirling her fork and stabbed a bit of bacon. "My folks are your typical parents, I guess. They were really strict when I was growing up, though. They almost shipped me off to a religious academy because they were worried about my attitude. They did ship me off to a Bible camp one year."

The pasta in his gut formed a knot as his own childhood abandonment ripped through him. "They gave you away?"

"No," she said hastily. "Nothing like that. Camp is supposed to be an opportunity for kids to have fun. Or, in my case, correct my behavior."

"What was wrong with your behavior?"

"I was kind of wild as a kid." She took a big drink of her margarita. "I rebelled a lot, especially if I was expected to participate in a church event."

He thought about that. Religion was a big thing in Sheoul, the difference being that most demons worshipped Satan. But he did know that, like humans, many didn't believe in any deity, while others participated in many of the varying human religions.

"Do they know what you do for a living now? Investigating demons for DART?"

"Do they ever," she said. "They're proud of me for being one of 'God's warriors.'"

He watched her take another drink. "Do they know about Jillian and Reseph?"

She coughed. Hard. "Oh, hell, no." She coughed again and cleared her throat. "They think he's a history professor from Europe who Jillian met when he came to Colorado on vacation. That's how I explain why they live there."

That made sense. "How do you explain me?"

"You're a friend who is renting her place."

A friend. Obviously, it wasn't the case. He'd never even had a friend.

"I wish that was true."

"Jillian doesn't consider you a...what the bond makes you. You *are* a friend, Tracker." She laid her hand on top of his and lightly stroked his skin. He liked it when she did that. "You're my friend, for sure."

She'd said that before, but he'd thought she was merely being nice. This time, a fizzy, warm sensation that had nothing to do with the alcohol spread through his veins. He wasn't sure what "normal" was for humans, but he'd seen enough stuff on TV to think that this might be pretty close.

Feeling unbelievably blessed, he dug into his dinner, and when the last of the food was gone, he sat back in his chair with a satisfied sigh. "That was the best meal I've ever eaten."

He wasn't only talking about the food. It was the company, too. When he lived in Sheoul, he either ate by himself or with other slaves, and since coming to Jillian's, he'd mostly eaten alone. She frequently invited him to eat with her and Reseph, and he was always welcome at their cookouts with family and friends. But he'd never felt comfortable no matter how friendly everyone had been.

Stacey took a sip of her drink and waggled her brows. "Oh, baby, I have so much to teach you."

"About cooking?"

"About anything you want."

Anything? In the background, the TV was still blaring music, which gave him an idea. From a show he watched sometimes. The margarita gave him the courage to speak the idea out loud. "Can you teach me to dance?"

She put down her glass and stared at him. "Are you serious?"

"Is that wrong?"

"No! Of course not. Dancing is one of my favorite things. How about a lesson right now?"

Now?

"Come on." Standing, she held her hand out to him. "We'll start with something super easy."

His mouth was dry as she pulled him into the living room and took his other hand so they were facing each other on the hardwood floor. She was inches away from him, so close he thought he could hear her heart beat if not for the music.

It was moments like this he'd been afraid to dream of, had never thought would happen. Not in a million years, and somewhere in his brain was the passing thought that he was crossing some sort of forbidden boundary. But before he could rethink it, Stacey moved to center them on the floor, and he was forced to follow.

"This is called a waltz. It's just four steps." She placed one of his hands on her waist and took the other in her own hand before resting her palm on his shoulder. "I'm going to lead, and our moves will form a box. I'll move forward one step with my left foot. You move back with your right." She demonstrated, and he followed along to her softly rhythmic "One, two, three. One, two, three. Relax and feel it in your body."

It didn't take long to settle into a routine, and gradually he did relax, letting himself move to the music. Once again, the effervescent warmth filled his body, and truly, he'd never enjoyed himself more. This female was magic. And who knew how wonderful music could be?

He looked down at her, the way her shoulder-length, shiny hair curled around her slender neck and framed eyes the color of a honed steel blade. He'd always viewed her as a fighter, and this domestic, sensual side of her surprised him in the best way. "How did you learn to do this?"

"To dance?" A soft blush bloomed in her cheeks. "I wanted to be a professional dancer when I was a kid. I entered competitions and everything."

Dancing with the Stars was one of his favorite shows—not that he'd admit it to anyone—and he tried to picture her on stage like the women who competed. She'd look like a goddess in a skimpy dress, her full breasts filling out a low-cut bodice, her legs going forever all the way from sexy high-heels to a flimsy skirt that would flutter during dips and twirls to reveal her curvy backside.

Oh, yeah. He could see her like that. But it struck him that he didn't want other males to see it, and he had to suppress a possessive growl at the very thought.

"Why didn't you become a dancer?"

"We don't really live in dance competition central, you know? The good schools are a long ways away, and my parents couldn't afford to take me to the big competitions in other states." She shrugged. "Plus, I don't have the body type for it."

She was so wrong. She had the body for anything, and his cock jerked in agreement.

"So what did you do instead?"

"I followed in my dad's footsteps and became a cop."

He nodded. "I saw you in a uniform once. Did you like it?"

"You know, I never really did. I was kind of directionless, so I did what a lot of kids do, and I carried on the family tradition. My grandpa was a cop, too." She stopped moving and smiled. "Now you lead. Start with your left foot and move forward."

Dancing definitely did not come naturally to Tracker—give him weapons or tools any day—but after stumbling a couple of times, he figured it out.

But he wasn't going to be on *Dancing with the Stars* anytime soon.

"So what made you leave the job?"

She blew out a long breath. "Wow. Well, my worldview was shaken when the whole almost-apocalypse thing happened, and I decided I was tired of domestic disturbances and cattle disputes between ranchers. So I joined DART, and now I handle the occasional demon sighting here."

One, two, three. One, two, three. "Is this what people do when they dance? Talk?"

"Sometimes. Would you like to stop?"

"No." He wanted to do this forever. Just lock out the rest of the world and do nothing but sway to the pulse of soft tunes.

As if she could read his thoughts, her gaze locked onto his. Held it. Those gray eyes, the color of new chains, captured him and pulled him closer.

He'd never been so glad to be chained.

Time, and the dance, came to a grinding halt as she went up on her toes, bringing her face closer to his. Awareness sizzled in the air around them, hot and potent. Desire and instinct collided, and without thinking, he dipped his head. In a heartbeat, their lips were nearly touching, separated only by a whisper.

His heart pounded so fiercely he swore his ribs might crack. He wanted to kiss her, wanted to feel something he'd never experienced before. Already it was a night of many firsts, but maybe he was pushing his luck. Maybe it was all too much.

Slaves weren't meant to have this kind of freedom, and while he knew that a *malibite* wasn't going to pop out of the woodwork, his body wasn't so sure.

Just as the soft skin of her lips touched his, he reared back, ruining everything.

Chapter 6

Idiot!

Inside her head, Stacey cursed herself for moving too fast. Things had felt so right. So natural. The moment had been perfect. But clearly, Tracker didn't share that opinion.

Humiliation shrank her skin, and she dropped her hands to her sides. "I'm sorry if I made you uncomfortable."

"You didn't." He looked pained, his eyes a little wild as he inhaled a shaky breath. "I just don't…I've never…"

"You never kissed anyone?"

When he shook his head, she kicked herself for her stupid question, because duh, he'd been a slave his entire life. When would he have gotten the chance to have a relationship?

But then, she didn't know if relationships were actually an option in his culture. Did slaves breed other slaves? She wanted to ask, but…how did one go about it? As far as delicate and awful subjects went, she couldn't think of any that were more so.

"Tracker, I don't want you to do anything you don't want to do. I would never force you."

"You wouldn't have to." The husky, raw honesty in his voice stole her breath.

"Then let me kiss you." She reached out and took his hand. "You've dealt with so much misery. Let me show you the very opposite."

She waited a torturously long time for his head to dip in a cautious nod of permission, and then she stepped closer, slowly, as if she were approaching a stray dog. Which was funny, given that he was a werewolf.

Oh, God, she was about to make out with a werewolf.

The thought sent a hot bolt of anxiety through her, and he suddenly stepped back again.

"Tracker?"

Sadness flared in his eyes, followed by a sudden sheen of ice as the defenses he'd lowered tonight went up once more. "You're afraid of me."

"What? No, I—"

"I can smell it," he growled, yanking his hand away.

"It's not fear," she swore.

"Then I disgust you."

She reached out and captured his wrist before he could retreat further. "That's not it at all. It's just…your world, the supernatural world, is pretty new to me. I'm a little nervous. I've only kissed humans."

Wow, that was a strange thing to say.

"So we're both nervous?"

Nervous? Seemed like a mild word for what she was feeling. "I guess so."

His gaze drilled into her so fiercely she felt like she was undergoing an interrogation with a polygraph examiner. "Do you wish I was human?"

"I don't wish you were anything but what you are. Trust me," she muttered. "Being human doesn't automatically make someone a good person. I've kissed a lot of humans who turned out to be terrible representations of the species."

"You've kissed a lot of humans?" The underlying jealousy in his tone made her blink.

And gave her warm fuzzies.

"More than I'd care to admit. But they're in the past. Right now, there's only you."

Hoping he wouldn't notice that her palms were sweating, she cupped his cheek, and her heart melted when he leaned into her touch. Slowly, so as not to spook him, she went up on her tiptoes and touched her lips to his. He stiffened, but at least this time he didn't back away. She let him get used to the sensation before increasing the pressure.

"Are you okay?" she whispered against his mouth, and at his shallow nod, she tugged him more firmly against her.

He leaned into it now, and when she flicked her tongue against the seam of his lips, he gasped, allowing her to deepen the kiss. He moaned at the invasion of her tongue, and she did too.

There were some serious sparks flying between them.

Encouraged, she lifted her other hand to his chest, feeling the beat of his pulse through his sweatshirt. It was strong and fast, and her own heart answered, tapping out a spastic message against her rib cage.

Oh, yeah. Sparky.

Then, as she was about to spice things up with a little nibble on his lower lip, the phone rang. He leaped away from her, his gaze flitting wildly around the room as if he was afraid someone was going to burst out of thin air and punish him.

By the second ring, he was calm again, so ice cold she wondered if she'd imagined the sparks.

"It's Jillian," he said, swiping the phone off the kitchen counter. "She sometimes calls in the evening." He answered with an impressively steady, "Hello," that gave no indication that just a moment ago he'd been as breathless as Stacey was. Apparently, Jillian asked for her, because he handed the phone to her right away.

"Hey." Stacey said. "What's up?"

"Nothing. I was just bored."

And you have terrible timing. "Sorry to hear that."

"What are you guys up to?"

Oh, nothing much. I was making out with your werewolf.

"Tracker and I just finished with dinner. We made something out of Suzanne's cookbook. And Tracker had his first margarita."

"*You gave him alcohol?*"

Uh-oh. Stacey flinched at the shrill note in Jillian's voice and moved to the bedroom for a little privacy.

"He *is* an adult," she said, lowering her own voice and hoping Tracker's super-hearing was dampened by said alcohol. "I mean, he's older than we are."

"I know, but…I don't know." Jillian sounded mildly frustrated, her words short and snappy. "Just be careful, Stacey. He's not used to our ways."

"Well, maybe it's time he got introduced to some of them." There was a moment of silence, and great, Jillian was probably mad at her. Shit. This wasn't how Stacey had wanted things to go. "Jillian? Are you okay?"

"Yeah. Yeah, of course. I just worry about him."

"Don't you trust me?"

"Stacey! Of course I do. I'm sorry. Like I said, I worry about him."

Totally understandable, she supposed. Stacey could only imagine how she'd handle being responsible for someone who was supernaturally bonded to her. "Can I ask you something?"

"Sure."

Stacey hesitated for a moment, wondering if she was crossing a line into Nunya. But she and Jillian had been friends for decades. Had shared everything from news of their very first periods to when and how they'd lost their virginity.

Stacey had never looked at the bed of a Chevy pickup the same way again.

Somehow, though, the topic of Tracker seemed even more personal.

"Why did you leave him here instead of taking him with you and Reseph when you moved?"

Jillian sighed. "I wanted to give him a chance at a life. With me and Reseph, he'd just think of himself as a slave. Why do you ask?"

"Because I don't think he feels like he's allowed to have a life of his own. It sounds like he needs permission for everything."

"Did he tell you that?"

"Not exactly." Stacey sank down on the bed and looked out the window at the falling snow. It wasn't coming down nearly as hard as it had been. "It's some of the things he's said."

"Sounds like you're really getting to know him."

Stacey had known Jillian almost her entire life, and for the first time, she couldn't read the tone of her voice. And she wasn't sure how to respond.

"Well," she hedged, "we *are* kind of trapped in a cabin together."

"Be careful, Stace." Again with the tone, and now Stacey felt her defensiveness creeping in.

"I don't know what you mean."

"I think you do," Jillian bit out. "He's not available."

Stacey sat there, momentarily stunned. She hadn't exactly expected Jillian's blessing to date Tracker, but she didn't think she needed it, either. She genuinely cared about him, and it was clear they shared a mutual attraction.

"Jillian—"

"I have to go. I'll talk to you later."

The line went dead. Stacey closed her eyes and exhaled. Dammit. She and Jillian had never fought. They'd never even had a minor spat. But for some reason, this felt like a fight. Like Jillian didn't trust Stacey.

Anger sparked a rebellious little fire in her. Tracker deserved more than a life of loneliness. Obviously, Jillian didn't want that for him, either. But how dare she forbid Stacey from helping him find it? It wasn't like she was some sort of underworld floozy succubus who was out to steal his soul or anything. It was just a kiss, for Heaven's sake.

But you wanted more.

Yeah, and so what? She hadn't been with a guy in over a year. And from the sounds of it, Tracker hadn't been with a woman—willingly, at least—ever.

Jillian was just going to have to accept that Tracker could make his own decisions.

So, with Jillian's warning ringing in her ears, she stood and headed to the living room. Where she found Tracker on the couch. Sound asleep and snoring.

Jillian had gotten her way after all.

Chapter 7

The storm was finally over. Tracker looked up at the brilliant blue sky and let the sun bathe his face. He never took days like this for granted. After living for most of his life in the demon underworld, he'd never not appreciate the beauty of a sunny day.

That said, he could live without the three feet of fresh snow that was sitting on top of the eighteen inches of snow that was already on the ground. Digging out of this mess was going to take days.

He looked out at the winter wonderland…which wasn't accurate, since tomorrow it would be May…and wondered where to start first. Digging out his vehicle and the driveway would be a high priority, but so was clearing around the barn again so the animals could stretch their legs. He also needed to plow a path to the nearest Harrowgate in the forest. If he had to go somewhere, like get Stacey to a hospital, that would be the fastest and safest way to go.

Well, he'd have to knock her out first, but aside from that, it was pretty safe.

Stacey, on the other hand, was not safe. In less than forty-eight hours, she'd gotten him to do things he never thought he'd do and talk about things he'd never talked about.

And today he was full of anxiety over it.

As a slave, he was so beneath Stacey she might as well be a princess and he a beggar.

Still, his pulse kicked up when he thought about last night and the kiss they'd shared. It had been the most exciting experience of his life, and he'd never had as much fun as he'd had when she'd taught him to dance. For the first time, he'd felt close to someone. And not just close, but comfortable. She'd made him feel like an equal, and he'd forever be grateful for those precious few moments.

He'd checked in on her this morning, and she'd been sound asleep in his bed, the covers drawn up to her chin, but one shapely leg exposed, a blanket twisted up around her thigh. Something about the sight had sparked a deep, raw desire, and he'd clenched his fists before backing out of the room and closing the door.

How he'd wanted to climb into bed with her.

Putting aside those dangerous fantasies, he got to work, starting with the barn, and once the goats and donkeys were happily outside playing in the smaller of two fenced-in pastures, he shifted his focus to the driveway. To his annoyance, Stacey had dug out his truck while he'd been working on the barn.

She was supposed to be taking it easy, but he'd bit his tongue and let her do it because Jillian had ordered him to. Well, she hadn't exactly made it a command, but when his master made a suggestion like "Let Stacey do whatever she wants," it was an order. Jillian assured him that, as her best friend, she had her complete trust and it was okay if she wanted to rummage through her house for supplies or even stay there as long as she wanted to.

The latter thing…he had mixed feelings.

He liked having Stacey in his house. She filled a space that had been empty for too long. But as great as last night had been—so great that merely thinking about it made his stomach flutter—this was all new to him, completely uncharted territory, and having her in his cabin was also as stressful as it was amazing.

She wanted to talk. To have conversations. And she asked questions. Questions about his life and his past that he didn't know how to answer. He hated talking to Jillian about it, so how was he supposed to tell Stacey about the horrors of his existence?

He was so ashamed.

And the thing was, the shame was fairly recent. He'd lived his entire life under the belief that slavery was normal. That he was living his fated lot in life. It was a miserable lot, but he'd never believed that happiness was in the cards for him. He was meant to be a slave, and that was that. There was no sense in hoping for more. Or better.

Then Jillian came into his life. She'd given him freedom in every way possible, to the extent that she could. She'd given him a home, a vehicle, education, and a real shot at life.

For the longest time, he didn't trust it. He was afraid to be happy. But now the fear was gone.

He reconsidered that, because no, it wasn't gone. It was simply morphed into a new fear. Now he was afraid of losing it all.

So along with the happiness came fear and a deep sense of shame when he was asked about his past. Humans seemed to have a visceral abhorrence for slavery, and whenever he talked about his experiences or his masters, the disgust and anger they felt burned right into his skin.

He'd been part of something ugly—still was part of it—and he didn't know how to shed that. Or to make people stop being horrified by him.

His mind churned with the dilemma as he plowed a path to the Harrowgate a few hundred yards from the cabins. The tractor cut through the snow effortlessly, but as he drew close to the gate, he slowed the rig to a crawl, his senses tingling with unease.

The gate, invisible to most humans, hung like a sparkly curtain between two big pines. In front of it, the snow was churned up. He stopped the plow and hopped out.

Two sets of footprints had torn up the area, but it looked like the owners had pretty much stepped out, realized that they weren't going anywhere in three feet of fresh snow, and left. Was this the origin of the unsettling sensation he'd felt last night?

No one came here accidentally. The maps inside the gates were well-marked and obvious to the users, no matter their species or language.

Someone had come for a reason.

And he was sure it wasn't for anything good.

* * * *

Stacey sank down on the couch with one of Suzanne's cookbooks, a couple of aspirin she'd snagged from Jillian's medicine cabinet, a mug of hot cocoa, and an ice pack around her ankle. She'd spent hours shoveling snow, and she'd definitely overdone it. Not that she was going to tell Tracker that. He was already annoyed enough at her for doing anything at all.

She turned on the TV and flipped through the available apps. Looked like Jillian—or, more likely, Reseph—had set Tracker up with just about everything possible, from HBO and Starz to Amazon Prime,

Netflix, Hulu, and even Disney Plus. She'd been bingeing *The Walking Dead*, but she felt like trying something new. And less dark.

She surfed for a while, settling on *The Santa Clarita Diet.* Looked cute, and who didn't love Drew Barrymore and Timothy Olyphant?

And she'd still get her zombie fix.

With one eye on the show and one in the cookbook, she mentally categorized the recipes into *YES, if we can scrounge up the ingredients*; *YES, we have all the ingredients, but I don't like at least one of them*; and *NO, for various reasons.*

She glanced up at the TV and laughed, her finger hovering over the ingredient list for cottage pie. Who would have known that Timothy Olyphant was so funny?

Back to the recipe. It looked like cottage pie was a winner. *Winner, winner, ground beef dinner.* Her mom had always said that when she made anything with hamburger…but never chicken.

The front door opened, and Tracker came in, stomping clumps of snow off his boots.

"Hey," she said. "How was your day?"

He bent to unlace his boots, and holy mother of Carhartt, he had a nice ass. "What?"

"How was your day?" *That ass.* "You know, what did you do?"

He straightened. "Why?"

That front. He filled out his jeans well *everywhere.* "Because I'm curious. It's one of those things people do. Share their day."

"Oh." He kicked off his boots and started on his parka. "Do you want me to list the things I did?"

He was so adorable. "How about if you share the things that were important to you. The good things. The bad things. Any things."

The coat tree groaned when he hung his jacket, leaving him in the peel-me-open-with-your-teeth jeans, a blue flannel button-down shirt, and gray socks. "I'm not used to that."

"What, small talk?"

"When my master asks questions, I give…"

"The bare minimum?"

"The most concise answer." He strode to the kitchen to get a bottle of water from the fridge. "It's what I was taught."

But not by Jillian. She wanted to remind him of that, but since last night there'd been a new energy between them, one they hadn't yet discussed or felt out. It would probably be best to keep things light for now.

"Well," she said as she casually moved the ice pack aside where he wouldn't notice, "when a human engages in small talk or asks you a personal question, they want more than the bare minimum."

He wrenched the cap off the water and tossed it into the garbage. "What if there are things I don't want them to know?"

Now *she* wanted to know.

Or did she?

"You're entitled to privacy, Tracker. If someone asks you something, they genuinely want your answer, but you don't have to say anything you don't want to say." She paused. "Unless they say in passing, 'How are you?' That's a greeting people just throw out there and no one really gives a shit." She leaned forward on the couch cushion and wrapped her fingers around the warm mug of cocoa. "So let's try this again. How was your day?"

He tipped the bottle to his lips and drank half the contents before speaking.

"I cleared the barnyard so the animals could go outside. Then I plowed the driveway with the tractor. It needed gas before I finished, so I filled the tank. After I filled the tank, I added oil too. Then I cleared the rest of the driveway, but the road down the mountain hasn't been plowed yet."

She hid a smile in her hot cocoa. He wasn't very good at the conversational stuff, obviously, but he'd get better.

"And I plowed a path to the Harrowgate in case there's an emergency." He paused, and her cop sense flared.

He was trying to decide if he should share something.

"Tracker? What is it?"

He emptied the water bottle, buying himself more time. "I found fresh tracks around the gate."

Didn't seem like a big deal. "Animal?"

"Boots."

That seemed like a bigger deal. "Did they lead anywhere?"

"Whoever it was turned around and went back, but I think there were at least two sets of prints."

Well, that was troubling. And her handy-dandy demon fighting gear was in her Jeep. Which was at the bottom of a ravine.

"I don't suppose you have a cache of weapons around here?"

"Not really. Just some axes, hatchets, and knives," he said, and she wondered what the hell he considered weapons, if not those things. "But Reseph keeps a trunk of weapons in their basement. He gave me permission to use them if needed."

"Maybe we should grab them."

He jerked his chin toward the back door. "They're already on the deck. I'll bring them inside and then hit the shower."

Well, wasn't he quite the prepared little werewolf. "While you're doing that, I'll get the ingredients together for dinner. I saw ground beef and mixed vegetables in your freezer, so tonight we're making cottage pie. We'll have to use Jillian's box of potato flakes instead of fresh potatoes, but it'll be fine. Then I'm teaching you a new dance."

As he reached for the doorknob, his smile was sexy and flirty, and all the more seductive because he had no idea he was doing it. "Only if you teach me to lead from the beginning."

"Anything you want, Tracker."

With that look, he could lead her anywhere.

Chapter 8

Tracker was a nervous wreck as he soaped up in the shower. Was it normal to feel like your insides were trying to escape through your pores? Did all males feel that way around females like Stacey? Hot, sexy, females who did nice things and offered even nicer things?

Anything you want, Tracker.

Did she understand what she'd said? Because if she knew what he wanted, he doubted she'd have said that.

His erection bobbed under the hot water as if agreeing.

Soapy water sluiced down his body, and he couldn't help but imagine it was her tongue creating the tingly sensations instead. He'd never had a female's tongue on him, at least, not in a sexual way. In the past, if anyone put their mouths on him, it was to cause pain or to drink his blood.

For once, he wanted the experience to be a good one.

In what felt like a split second, his gut churning in anticipation, he rinsed, toweled dry, and dressed in black sweat pants and a black and brown fitted flannel button-down shirt Reseph had gotten him. Another one of those items he said women liked.

He combed his hair, thinking he should have gotten it cut. And maybe he should shave. His werewolf genes meant he didn't have to shave more than once a week and he'd shaved yesterday, but what if his face was too rough? Should he brush his teeth again?

He stared at himself in the mirror because what the fuck? He'd never obsessed about his looks. And he wasn't going to start now.

Although he really should cut his hair.

When he was done obsessing, he found Stacey already preparing dinner.

"Hey," she said, not turning around. "I'm just doing the prep work. I'll show you all the steps in the cookbook and we'll work on identifying the ingredients." She looked over her shoulder at him and smiled. "Nice shirt. Color looks good on you."

"What about my hair?"

"What?"

"Nothing. Whatever you're doing smells good."

"It's the chopped onion." She gestured him over and pointed to a word in the cookbook he didn't recognize. "See that?"

He sounded it out in his mind, and then what she'd said made sense. "Minced. Onion."

"Yes! And the next ingredient is—"

"Wait," he said. "Don't say anything." Inspired by Stacey's enthusiasm, he worked it out in his head. He already knew numbers and measurements, so the tablespoon part was easy. "One tablespoon tomato paste."

"You got it."

Great. But he'd never seen it before in his life. "I don't have tomato paste."

She pointed to a tiny can on the counter. "Jillian had some in her pantry."

He read the rest of the recipe, and they worked on dinner for the next half an hour. Every once in a while, he'd pause, struck by what was happening. This was normal life. Preparing food *with* someone, not *for* someone. Someone who might beat you if the dish wasn't seasoned to his liking.

As he handed her the bowl of mashed potatoes, he realized that as great as his life had been for the last few years, it could be even better.

And it was all because of Stacey.

A sudden urge to push her up against the fridge and kiss her, bite her, mark her as his, was so intense he had to grip the counter and focus on the food. Not her slender hands as they smoothed the potatoes on top of the meat mixture. Not her breasts and how they filled out the black V-neck sweatshirt. And definitely not her full, fine ass when she bent over to slip the cottage pie into the oven.

Dragging his palm over light stubble he should have shaven off, he pivoted away from her and gathered dishes to set the table. Stacey poured red wine into two long-stemmed glasses that must have come from Jillian's house.

"Have you ever had wine before?" she asked as she handed him a glass. It felt so delicate in his big, calloused hand.

"Not human wine." He eyed the dark liquid and casually adjusted the glass so he was holding it around the base, like Stacey, and not by the stem. "I'm guessing it's not made with blood or marrow, like the stuff in Sheoul."

"Aaaand...you just gave me reason number eight thousand and twelve to be glad I grew up in the human realm. Ugh." She grimaced as she reached for the TV remote. "Do you miss Sheoul? I mean, I'm sure you don't miss most of it, but was there anything good about Sheoul? Anything at all?"

"No." His gut churned just thinking about it. "Everything there is ugly or poisonous. The plants, the animals, even the soil. It all wants to eat you."

"What about Harvester?"

His gut upped the churning routine with a slow somersault. "What about her?"

"I know she gave you to Jillian so you could have a better life, and she's a Heavenly angel now, so she couldn't have been really awful, right?"

"Yes...and no." He considered his answer carefully, since he had a complicated relationship with the former fallen angel. "She treated me better than my other masters. And she did give me to Jillian. And she gave me a summoning coin in case I ever need her. But..." He shrugged. The last thing he wanted to talk about was his old masters.

Stacey glanced toward the bedroom. "The coin on your dresser. Is that the one?"

He nodded. "I can't imagine ever using it. Seeing her would be another reminder of my past, and I want to forget."

"Well, then, I think we should watch something fun while we eat."

"We won't eat at the table?"

"Nope." She grabbed the remote. "Let's have dinner and a movie night."

He joined her on the couch, deciding he liked human normal. It was way better than demon normal.

She flipped through the apps and channels with a practiced touch.

"Do you like rom coms?"

"I love them." He had no idea what rom coms were, but he didn't care. Whatever made her happy would be fine with him.

"Really?" She gave him a skeptical lift of one golden brown eyebrow. Busted. "Have you seen *Ever After*?"

"Nope."

"*While You Were Sleeping*?"

"Nope."

"*You've Got Mail*?"

"No."

"*Pretty Woman*?"

Finally, one he'd seen. "Jillian watched it when I was staying in her spare bedroom before my cabin was built. Vivian was a succubus, right?"

Stacey laughed out loud. "Close enough." She scrolled some more. "Ooh, I know! *There's Something About Mary*. It's hilarious and so, so wrong."

He wasn't sure what was wrong about it, or why that would be a good thing, but he didn't really care. She started the movie and then scooted over on the couch so she was only inches from him, and his entire world seemed right. With her so close, he could feel her heat and hear her heartbeat, and through the aroma of beef and onion cooking in the oven, he could smell the piney soap she'd used in his shower.

A primal surge of protectiveness and possession made him want to sweep her up and carry her to his bed. The urge hit him hard, a rattling, deep tremor so powerful he kind of dazed out. For a moment, he couldn't figure out what the hell was going on, but once his brain engaged again, he got a dose of reality. The full moon was coming and with it, hyper-intense reactions to everything.

He slid a glance over at her, hoping she hadn't noticed anything. Thankfully, she was glued to the TV, laughing into her wine.

Damn, he wanted to kiss her again. He wanted her mouth on him, not the glass. He wanted his mouth all over her, kissing, licking—

The oven timer went off, saving him from doing something stupid.

Stacey paused the movie so they could dish up and settle back down on the couch.

The cottage pie was a big glop of savory goodness, and the movie was as funny as it was baffling. Humans were complex, strange, and surprisingly humorous. So much he'd learned about them in Sheoul was turning out to be lies.

He stole looks at Stacey often while they ate, committing all of this to memory. It was time to replace all the bad shit, and maybe these new memories would overwrite the old ones. The longer she was here, the more balanced his world would become.

He was actually starting to dread the roads opening up again.

When the movie was over and the credits started rolling, Stacey hiked a leg up on the cushion and turned to him with a bounce. "Did you like it?"

"I've never laughed so hard in my life," he admitted, feeling a buzz that had nothing to do with the alcohol.

"Good." Stacey clinked her glass against his. "You should laugh more."

She was so beautiful, her face flushed from laughing, her lips stained red from the wine, and he had to temper a purr of admiration that threatened to come out as an erotic growl of need.

"It's not just the movie." He hadn't been able to temper his voice, and his words came out in a dark, gravelly drawl.

"No?"

"No." He wasn't sure what to do now. His heart was pounding and his stomach was fluttering. All he knew was the truth. "It's you too."

The look in her eyes, one of raw heat, sparked something new in him. Something savage. Something hot.

Maybe it was the near-full moon. Maybe it was pure male instinct. Maybe it was a sense of freedom he was only now beginning to understand. Whatever it was, it demanded he finally take action.

He put down his glass and then, very slowly, very deliberately, he reached for her, sliding his hand around the nape of her neck as he leaned in and touched his mouth to hers.

* * * *

If Tracker hadn't told Stacey he'd never kissed anyone before, she wouldn't have believed it. He knew instinctively how much pressure to use at the right time. He knew how to hold her with the perfect mix of give and take, making her feel possessed, yet in control.

He tasted of wine and spice and male, a heady combination that made her moan as she slid her hand around his back so she could scoot even closer to him.

His tongue touched the seam of her lips in a tentative, probing tap, and before she gave in, she playfully nipped his lower lip. He sucked in a quick, sharp breath followed by a low growl that vibrated her all the way to her core.

She'd been with more guys than she was proud of, alpha males who had pushed all her buttons. Men who were proficient with weapons and women.

Tracker had just relegated them all to amateur hour.

"Tracker," she breathed, lifting his hand to her breast. "Touch me." She held him there as she arched into his palm. "Yes, right there."

His caress was light, as tentative as his kiss, but searing hot. When she pressed even closer and threw her leg across his lap, he shuddered and grew bolder, his touch firmer, his kiss more aggressive.

Desire pooled between her legs as he lunged, forcing her back into the cushions. His thigh pressed against her center, easing the ache that was starting to throb. She lifted her knee, brushing the fly of his pants and the hard ridge behind it, and he hissed.

"Wait," he breathed. "Wait." He pulled back, his lips wet from their kiss, his face flushed. "I can't. I need permission."

"You have it." She slid her hand around his neck to pull him back down. "I won't say no."

He reared away, breaking her hold. "My master. I need permission from my master."

Well, if that wasn't a bucket of ice water thrown on all her smoldering body parts.

"I already talked to Jillian about being with you." It wasn't *entirely* a lie. They had talked about Tracker. It's just that Jillian had said to stay away from him.

He hovered above her. "You did?"

"You came up in our conversation."

"And she gave her permission?"

"Well, not exactly, but—"

He shoved to his feet with a growl. "Then I can't. Kissing you was too much already."

Her frustration boiled over, frustration with his situation, his past, and yes, at Jillian too, and she shot to her feet with a curse.

"Dammit, this 'permission' crap is ridiculous. Jillian might hold your bond, but she doesn't own you. Not in this way," she added, when he opened his mouth to argue. "You're allowed to have fun. You're allowed to be yourself. You get to make your own choices. I don't care if your *master* forbade this, and neither should you."

"What?" his voice went low. And pissed. "*She forbade this*? And you still let me kiss you? And touch you? What if we'd—" He shook his head. "You…you…*succubus*."

Succubus? "That's a little harsh…"

Jamming his hand through his hair, he paced around the living room. "She will be furious with me. Don't you understand?"

"No, I don't understand," she yelled. "I don't understand why you won't fight for yourself. For your happiness. Jillian has basically freed you, but you keep putting the shackles back on."

He wheeled around, the fury in his eyes snapping like fire. "You dare speak of shackles? As if you know what it's like to be me?" His gaze shifted, going somewhere beyond her, as if he couldn't bear to look her in the face anymore. "Listen—"

"No, you listen, please." She had to make him see that he was worthy of a good life. A life of independence in which he didn't have to ask anyone for permission for anything.

"No. I mean, *listen*. Outside."

She hit the mute button on the TV remote. She didn't hear anything, but she didn't have supernatural werewolf senses. "If there's something out there, we should check it out."

"I'll do it." He yanked his jacket off the coat rack. "You stay here."

"Screw that." She tossed the remote to the couch and went for her own coat. "I'm a trained DART agent. I'm fully capable of—"

"You're injured. I saw the ice pack you tried to hide. Seems like you hide a lot from me." He shoved his feet into his boots before arming himself with an ax and a couple of blades. "Stay inside. I know the area, and I can see in the dark."

He had a point, but that didn't mean she was going to give in. "Fine. I'll go through the chest and itemize the weapons," she said, as if it were her idea to remain behind. "But if you're not back in ten minutes, I'm coming after you."

"No." He tugged open the door with a snarl that carried outside with the cold and echoed for an eerily long time. "My mistress will be angry if you get hurt on my watch."

"Yeah?" Ugh, she was so sick of the mistress shit. "She also said I can do whatever I want." She grabbed the phone. "Want me to call for *permission*?"

A muscle in his jaw twitched as he clenched it tight. Then, wordlessly, he pivoted on his heel, stormed outside, and slammed the door behind him.

And wow. Now she felt like a jackass.

Sighing, she eyed the weapons chest and hoped it contained a whole bunch of useful shit. Including an apology.

Chapter 9

Impossible female.

Damn, Stacey was stubborn.

And sure, Tracker liked that. To a point. Her stubbornness made it damned hard to protect her. As a DART agent, he was sure she was capable, just as she'd said. But just as *he'd* said, she was injured, and until he found out what they were dealing with, she had no business being out here.

It was his duty. Period.

As far as her deception—although he hesitated to label it that—he wasn't sure what to do. He didn't truly believe that Jillian would be cruel in her anger. His reaction had more to do with his past experiences than his present.

And in the past, he could be tortured mercilessly for what had happened between he and Stacey. Now…now he was worried more about disappointing Jillian.

Jillian has basically freed you, but you keep putting the shackles back on.

Shackles? Stacey had no idea.

But it was something he'd have to deal with later. Right now, something was lurking in the forest.

He looked toward the heavens, measuring the darkness. The sky was clear and the moon was nearly full. Which meant a lot of light. Too much light. He'd be easily seen out in the open.

The trees and buildings threw silhouettes onto the fresh white snow, so he kept between drifts and in the shadows as best as he could and used his natural night vision to scan the forest. Pausing near the barn, he raised his head, seeking scents that might be out of place.

He caught a whiff of a deer somewhere nearby, but aside from that, nothing stood out. Still, the sense of a threat remained, like an oil slick on his skin.

He moved cautiously in the direction of the Harrowgate. The roads weren't cleared yet, so anyone trying to get here would either have to use the gate, flash in, or hike for miles through deep snow and thick forest.

He really hoped no one had flashed in. Anyone capable of materializing into a location was powerful. Granted, anyone who could use a Harrowgate was a bigger threat than your average human, but the flashers were next-level dangerous. Fallen angel and hellhound-level dangerous.

As he approached the plowed path leading to the Harrowgate, the danger vibe intensified. Adrenaline spiked hot in his veins, bringing with it the high of the hunt. The only time he'd been happy in Sheoul was when there was a threat or when he was hunting something his masters wanted. The beast inside him craved the chase, and for a brief time, nothing else mattered. He could forget everything but the thrill of the hunt and the satisfaction of a good battle.

He'd given his all, and he'd earned a reputation among slave owners of being willing to face anything, do anything, go anywhere, because he was so brave.

His owners, who had bragged about his fierceness, were wrong. He hadn't been brave. He just hadn't cared whether he'd lived or died.

Now he cared.

More important, he had people he cared *about.*

He sniffed the air, and this time, he got a hit. A territorial rage spun up at the familiar scents of two males from his parents' pack. No one from his pack had ever come here. So why now?

Inhaling deeply, he followed the scent to fresh footprints made by two sets of boots.

And they were headed toward the cabin.

Stacey.

Gripping his ax tight, he ran toward home, and when the tracks veered off the plowed path and deeper into the woods, he kept to the trail, hoping to cut them off. They were probably going to sneak around back.

He put on a burst of speed, and as he reached the yard, the front door opened and Stacey stepped out.

"Get inside," he yelled. "Now."

Giving him a *kiss-my-ass* smirk, she held up an S-shaped, double-bladed Aegis weapon called a *stang* in one hand, and a pistol in the other. Bullets didn't do jack shit against most demons, but they could put a hurting on werewolves in human form.

Damn, she was as awesome as she was frustrating.

The smile fell off her face and her gaze shifted over his shoulder as the sound of crunching snow and breaking branches broke the silence. He wheeled around in time to see two figures, shrouded in the shadows of standing and dead trees, burst from around the side of the house and sprint toward the Harrowgate on the cleared trail.

Snarling, he gave chase. They had a fifty-yard head start, but he gained on them, running so hard his lungs burned. He was close now, so close he could practically touch them…almost there, almost to the gate…he dove at them…

Light flashed, and they disappeared into the Harrowgate. The gate sliced shut, and Tracker tumbled, empty-handed, between the trees and landed in a graceless angry heap.

Cursing, he shoved to his feet and brushed off clumps of snow.

Two days. He had two days until the full moon, and then he was going to visit his pack, and he was going to find out what the hell was going on.

Stacey met him on the trail halfway back to his cabin, her limp even more pronounced on the uneven ground. She'd holstered the firearm, but she still carried the *stang* with the confidence of someone who knew how to use it.

"That's an Aegis weapon." He passed her on the trail but slowed so she could match his gait. "Why do you know how to use one?"

"Kynan insists that DART members are capable with all kinds of weapons. You never know when an enemy weapon is all that's available to you." She shrugged. "Not that The Aegis is the enemy, but, you know."

Yeah, he knew. The Aegis, an ages-old demon-slaying organization, had split into two factions, one that was pretty much a humans-only club whose radical ideology operated on the premise that the only good demon was a dead demon, and one that recognized the shades of gray between good and evil. The latter faction became the Demonic Activity Response Team, and while The Aegis and DART weren't exactly enemies, they were definitely rivals.

"So, who were those guys?" Stacey tucked the *stang* away and shoved her hands into her coat pockets.

"Two of my pack members." Ludwig and Jack were gone, but he still scanned the forest for any remaining threat. "I don't know what they were doing, but I'm going to find out."

"Right now?"

"No." He cast a sideways glance at her. "Why?"

"Because we need to talk."

Talking was the last thing he wanted to do. He didn't even want to speak long enough to say no. It took him a full ten yards to finally grit out, "We really don't."

"But Tracker—"

"I said, no." Unspent anger clawed at the edges of his control. He'd been counting on a good fight at the end of the chase. In the past he'd tangled with Lud and Jack in beast form, and he could have taken them—if he was allowed to. As the lowest-ranking werewolf in the pack, he wasn't permitted to fight for dominance or rank. Any attempt would result in punishment, banishment, or worse.

But here, on his territory and in human form, all bets were off.

He wanted to draw blood *before* the talking, the explanation of why the two assholes had been skulking around.

Only after he'd dispersed a little tension did he want to deal with what was going on between him and Stacey.

Jillian.

Jillian was what was going on between him and Stacey. She was in control, and Stacey either mocked it or refused to acknowledge it.

Stacey jogged ahead of him and stopped to block his path. "Please."

He halted a foot away. The light from the front porch, magnified by the snow and the brightness of the moon, outlined her body in a golden glow. There was something wild about her, primitive and fierce, like she belonged in the forest and on the hunt.

She'd make an amazing werewolf.

But that didn't change the fact that he was still pissed, and he seized her by the shoulders and gently moved her aside.

"You mocked me tonight." He picked up his pace, figuring if he couldn't get her to stop talking, maybe he could outrun her.

"Mocked you?" Stacey caught up, but he remembered her hurt leg and slowed down again. So much for outrunning her. "How? I mean, I might not have been especially forthright about my chat with Jillian, and I'm sorry for that, but I would never make fun of you."

He started up the porch steps. "You have no respect for my bond with my master." He offered Stacey a hand, but it wasn't a surprise when she waved it away.

"Well…yeah. I have no respect for slavery." She brushed past him at the top of the stairs and opened the door. "It's depraved and ugly, and it deserves to be reviled."

"Agreed." He certainly wasn't going to argue with that. "But it's my entire world, Stacey. I don't have a choice. Jillian doesn't have a choice. There are rules I *have* to follow. They're bullshit rules, but breaking them means unimaginable pain. Some rules I'm compelled to obey because of the magic infused into the bond." He stepped inside with her and closed the door. "I literally can't kill myself, harm any master, or allow harm to come to one." He tossed the ax down with a little too much force, and it chipped the floor. Great. He had no idea how to fix that. "You think it's ridiculous that I want permission from my mistress for small things, but it's all I know. And you treat it like it's a joke."

"Oh, Tracker." Stacey straightened from untying her boot laces. "I didn't think of it that way. I didn't mean to—"

He held up his hand, cutting her off. "Can we do this later? I need to be alone right now. Put on my *shackles*."

The devastation in Stacey's expression nearly made him cave in. He wanted to grab her, hold her against him, and make the rest of the world disappear. But he'd wished the world away too many times during his life to know it would never happen.

"I'll go stay at Jillian's and get out of your way." She bent to tie her boots again.

"No," he said, taking her elbow to lift her up. "Stay here. I don't want my pack to come back and find you by yourself."

"Then let me take the couch tonight."

Not happening. "I'll take it. I want to be close to the doors."

For a long moment, he thought she would argue. But finally, just as shit started getting awkward, she took off her coat, slipped into the bedroom, and closed the door.

Chapter 10

Tracker was already outside working when Stacey got up the next morning, feeling like total crap.

When she'd come to bed, she'd been angry, mostly at herself, because Tracker had been right. She couldn't respect the bond, but she could respect Tracker and his situation. And maybe she'd been a little unfair regarding Jillian's role in his life.

What she had to do was find a happy middle, where Tracker could be "free" but still operate within the parameters of his bond with Jillian.

The shackles.

Feeling sick to her stomach, she showered and dressed in a pair of Jillian's jeans and one of her black turtlenecks, and had just finished her first glass of iced coffee when there was a knock at the door.

A *knock*.

She doubted the roads were open, and Tracker wouldn't knock on his own door.

Shit.

Heart pounding, she grabbed the *stang*, the cold metal feeling extra heavy in her hand today. Quietly and carefully, she eased up to the front window and peeked through a crack in the curtains as a familiar voice called out.

"Stace? You in there?"

Jillian?

Yup. Her friend was standing on the porch, shivering, in a pair of black leggings, summery leather flats, and a long midnight satin top. Her hands were clutching grocery bags, and clearly, she was freezing.

Stacey threw open the door. "Oh my gosh. What are you doing

here? Dressed like that?"

Jillian put down the bags and gave her a big hug as soon as the door was closed. "I left all my winter stuff here. I don't really need it in Athens."

Stacey gave her friend a good-natured roll of the eyes. "There you go, bragging about your world travel again."

Jillian bounced the eye roll back at her. "If you'd just let Reseph do it, he'd take you anywhere you want to go."

"No thanks," Stacey said. "I'll stick with good, old-fashioned human-built airplanes."

"Pfft." Jillian waved her hand. "Air travel is so yesterday."

Laughing because Jillian had gotten her pilot's license years ago in order to fly DART charters, Stacey drew back the curtains and looked for Reseph, but he must have been in the barn or out on the property. "I guess the crisis in Australia died down?"

Jillian shook her head, making her dark bob swing around her chunky silver necklace. "I asked Limos to bring me. She'll be back in an hour to pick me up." Stacey helped her carry the bags to the kitchen. "I figured that since you're snowed in, you could use some supplies. When Limos gets back, she can take you to your place if you want."

"It's okay. I can wait for the roads to be cleared."

"It's really no trouble," Jillian said with another casual wave of her hand, which looked freshly manicured, the shiny black nail polish glittering in the overhead light.

Stacey glanced over at her friend as she filled the tea kettle she'd brought from Jillian's place. "You might be used to traveling through magic portals cast by Biblical legends, but I'm not there yet."

"I get that." Jillian shoved one of the bags toward Stacey and started to unpack the other. "But it's really not bad."

"I'm fine here for a couple more days." Stacey put the kettle on the stove and lit the burner before starting on the bag. "I'm helping Tracker dig out and learn to cook."

"Suzanne already worked with him."

"I know, but he has trouble with some of the ingredients in the cookbooks."

Jillian shoved a few food items into the refrigerator. "I'm sure Suzanne can come back to help him out."

Stacey got the feeling that Jillian was actively discouraging her from staying until the roads cleared. With a huff, she slammed the box of tea down on the counter.

"Okay, Jillian...just say it. Are you trying to get me away from Tracker?"

Jillian pursed her lips. She was sporting a bright red shade of lipstick Stacey had always wanted to wear but that made her look like a washed-out vampire. It was peach tones or nothing for her pale complexion.

"I guess I'm a little overprotective. Physically, he can take care of himself. But for as old as he is, and for as rough of a life as he's had, he's still naïve about a lot of things." She paused, tapping her nails on the counter. "And your dating history is kind of messy."

Frowning, Stacey fetched two cups from the cupboard. "What are you talking about?"

"Seriously? You dumped almost every guy you dated. They were too short or too tall or too dumb or too smart—"

Stacey gasped in mock outrage as she swung around to her friend. "Oh, come on. None of them were too smart."

Jillian cocked a dark eyebrow. "Matthew?"

Okay, there was Matthew. But... "It wasn't that he was too smart. It was that he was super smart and liked everyone to know it."

Jillian laughed. "God, he was obnoxious."

"So obnoxious." He'd spent every minute of their relationship talking about himself. "Come on, Jillian. You know I'm not willing to waste my time with a guy when it's clear we don't click. I tell it like it is. Brutal honesty."

"You totally got that from your parents." Jillian dropped a couple of tea bags into the mugs, and her expression turned serious. "I just don't want to see Tracker hurt. You're not used to his world, and he's a—"

"Slave?"

"I was going to say werewolf." She poured steaming water from the kettle into each of the waiting cups. "But yeah, that's a concern too."

Stacey propped her hip against the counter and eyed Jillian as she dipped her tea bag in and out of the water. "How can you stand it?"

"Stand what?"

"*Owning* someone."

"You make it sound like I had a choice. I didn't. Tracker was forced on me, Stacey. Do you think I *want* a slave? Would you want him?"

As a slave? "Hell no. Never."

"Believe me, if I could give him up, I would."

Stacey stood there for a second, stunned. "You mean, give him to someone else?"

Jillian looked taken aback. "No. Oh, God, never. I know that with me he'll have a good life. As good as I can give him, anyway. I meant that if I could give up his bond so he could have freedom, I would." She took a seat at the table, and Stacey joined her.

"I guess I don't understand why, if you own him, you can't free him."

Looking down at her mug of tea, Jillian shook her head. "Reseph explained that my ownership is more like a lease. Except I didn't sign anything and I don't know all the terms. He thinks I'm in violation just because I'm human, and if that's the case, we're lucky the slavers haven't found out yet."

Stacey went cold all over. "What happens if they find out?"

"They could take him away from me. But don't worry," she said, even though there was a note of concern in her voice. "Reseph won't let that happen."

Unless Reseph was away at some disease-ridden scene of tragedy, like he was now.

"So, what's going on with you two?" Jillian asked in a not-so-subtle attempt to change the subject.

Stacey played innocent. "What do you mean?"

Jillian gave her the don't-bullshit-me look she had perfected since high school. "You're blushing and fidgeting. Something's going on."

There was no sense in denying Jillian's accusation, and truthfully, it would be great to have someone to talk to about this. Even if her friend disapproved of what was going on between Stacey and Tracker.

"We kind of had a fight last night," she admitted. "Totally my fault. I want him to see that he has all this freedom, but he insists he needs permission from you to do anything."

Jillian paused with her mug halfway to her mouth. "He doesn't need permission for anything except going to Sheoul. I've told him that."

"I know. It's infuriating." She blew steam off the cup of tea. "Which is where I screwed up. And I did something I shouldn't have done."

Very slowly, Jillian put her mug down and shot Stacey a look that made her squirm. "What did you do?"

"Well, I was kind of mad at you…"

"And?"

More squirming. "And I kind of implied that you were okay with stuff."

"What kind of stuff?"

"It was just a kiss."

"A kiss," she echoed with a frown. "That's it?"

Stacey bit down on her bottom lip and finally ponied up the rest of the story. "Well, there was a little messing around. But that's all, I swear."

"Dammit, Stacey, I told you—"

"I know what you told me," Stacey snapped, instantly on the defensive. "But do you want him to be happy? Because I don't think he is. I think he's basically existing. Waiting for the next horrible thing around the corner."

Jillian sat there in stunned silence. "Are you sure?"

"I am." Stacey fiddled with her tea bag for a second, searching for words she probably wouldn't find in the hot brew. She wanted Jillian's approval, and not just because Tracker needed it. Her friend meant everything to her, and she didn't want anything to come between them. Especially not a man. Or a werewolf. "But Jillian, he laughs around me. He's starting to talk. I think I'm good for him. I really do."

"I've never seen him laugh," Jillian murmured as she stared into her mug. "I thought giving him space was what was best. He always seemed so uncomfortable around me and Reseph."

"That's because you *own* him. He lives to please you, no matter how much you tell him he doesn't need to. But around me, he can relax."

Tears welled in Jillian's eyes. "Shit. I didn't realize. Or maybe I didn't want to." She dabbed at the tears with the back of her hand. "I've been selfish, haven't I? I think I was cool with taking off with Reseph and leaving Tracker here because I didn't want to see what was so obvious. I didn't want to deal with owning someone, you know?"

Stacey reached out and took her friend's hand, hating seeing her in pain and feeling guilty for ever thinking the situation was anything less than awful for Jillian. "I can't even imagine what you've gone through."

Jillian smiled sadly and squeezed Stacey's fingers. "You're such a good friend. I'm sorry if I—" Her phone dinged and she looked down at the text. "It's Limos. She'll be here to pick me up in a second. Oh, and before I forget, I brought you a new phone." She dug through her purse and pulled out a silver iPhone. "It's got your old number on it."

"Oh my God, thank you. I'll pay you back—"

"It's a gift."

"But—"

"Don't worry about it. Really. Reseph and the other Horsemen are like, made of money."

"Still, this is too much."

"No, it's not. I appreciate what you're doing for Tracker, and I feel bad for being such a jerk about it. I'm so sorry."

"You weren't a jerk," Stacey said. "You were concerned. Never apologize for that. *I'm* sorry for not understanding where you were coming from."

"It's all okay." Jillian eased to her feet, and Stacey stood with her. "Are we good?"

"We're great. I love you."

"I love you too." Jillian gave Stacey a big hug. "And you have my blessing if you want to be with Tracker."

Relief and joy and all the good emotions filled Stacey with a new sense of determination.

Until she remembered Tracker's fury and realized that Jillian's blessing might have come too late.

Chapter 11

Anger and hurt circulated through Tracker's veins like lit gasoline as he worked on the damage to the barn's roof he'd discovered when he'd cleared it of snow.

He'd sensed Jillian's return earlier, and he'd gone to his cabin to see if there was anything she needed. But at the door, he'd overheard her conversation with Stacey.

"You make it sound like I had a choice. I didn't. Tracker was forced on me, Stacey. Do you think I want a slave? Would you want him?"

"Hell no. Never."

"Believe me, if I could give him up, I would."

Like an abused farm dog, he'd retreated to the barn, feeling like he'd been whipped until his skin was broken and bleeding.

No, not his skin. His heart. He'd known that his bond had been transferred to Jillian against her will, but to hear her say it like that…it shredded him like nothing else.

She wanted to give him up. What if she did? He loved it here. He loved the freedom he had. For the first time in his life, he lived without inhaling fear with every single breath.

He'd never allowed himself to have an opinion. Or to hope. Or to care about his fate. But now he had opinions and hope and a will to live, and he finally gave a shit about what happened to him.

If he lost all of that…he didn't know what he'd do.

It occurred to him that what Jillian had done with kindness was far worse than any cruelty his past masters had inflicted on him.

As he nailed a board across a gap in the rafters, the ever-present awareness of the slave bond grew rubbery, stretching as his master went on the move, and then it abruptly settled into a faint twinge, and he knew she was gone. In a way, he hoped she'd taken Stacey with her.

Would you want him?

Hell, no.

Hell, no.

Heart aching, he climbed down from the ladder and grabbed a pitchfork as the barn door opened. Assuming it was Stacey, he turned, dreading the confrontation.

It wasn't Stacey.

Instantly, a snarl dredged from deep in his chest at the sight of the two big males in winter gear in the doorway. Dammit, if he hadn't been so distracted by his thoughts, he'd have sensed them long before this.

"Hey, Tracker." Ludwig, the head enforcer from Tracker's pack, slipped inside like a lean, seven-foot tall ghost, his silver-white hair curling around his ears from under a white stocking cap.

His lieutenant, Jack, followed behind, a shorter, stouter, darker version of Lud in that they were both assholes even if they were, physically, the exact opposite of each other.

"I guess you decided to show your faces instead of slinking around the property."

Jack shrugged. "We had to be sure this was where you live."

Bullshit. They were doing reconnaissance.

"You're damned lucky I didn't catch you last night."

They ignored that. "We have news." Lud gestured for Jack to close the door. "Your parents are dead," he announced in a blunt, grave voice.

Tracker didn't give a shit. His parents had traded him and their souls for a chance to lead the pack, and he owed them nothing. They deserved nothing. Not a single fucking tear.

"And?"

Jack looked up from peering inside the empty livestock stalls, and Tracker was suddenly glad the goats and donkeys were outside. "Show some respect, worm. They were your sire and dam."

"Am I supposed to mourn the people who made my life a living hell? Fuck that."

"It was for the good of the pack," Jack said. "Their sacrifice allowed us—"

"*Their* sacrifice?" Tracker laughed, a bitter, hard sound. "Seems to me I'm the one who paid the price while they reaped the rewards."

When Jack opened his mouth to speak, Lud held up his hand, staying him. "It doesn't matter." He turned to Tracker. "When your mother sold you, it was to keep our pack whole and healthy as long as she or her descendants were pack leaders."

"I'm failing to see what this has to do with me. I have two brothers and a sister."

"No, you don't. They were all killed with your parents."

Tracker drew in a sharp breath. "All?" That didn't seem likely. "How?"

Jack snarled. "Aegis scum."

"Huh." Once again, Tracker was finding it hard to dredge up any sympathy. His siblings had treated him like he had mange, as if close proximity to him would result in their own slavery. "Well, thanks for the heads-up. Best of luck with the pack."

Jack came toward him like a bull, stopping a couple of feet away, his dark eyes blazing. "The pack will suffer without a leader with *Volgy* lineage."

With his siblings dead, the *Volgy*, the most ancient of the Hungarian warg bloodlines, now ended with Tracker.

Too bad.

"I know you're not suggesting that I lead the pack."

"Hardly." Lud laughed, because that was just the kind of dick he was. Dick protégé Jack snickered. "This is about Victoria."

Victoria...the sleek redhead who worked as a human dental assistant? She'd never been cruel to him, but she'd never been that friendly, either. "Why?"

"We want you to mate with her."

It was Tracker's turn to laugh. Surely they weren't serious. But Ludwig continued with the insanity.

"Once she's pregnant, she can lead the pack until the cub is born and old enough to take over."

"Nice try, boys," Tracker said, not bothering to hide his amusement at their desperation. "But I'm sterile."

"Not a problem." Jack tucked his gloved hands into his jacket pockets. "We've already been to the slaver guild. Your sterility is reversible."

Tracker's amusement veered sharply to unease. If they'd gone to the *malibites,* Tracker was back on their radar. Which was never, *ever*, a good thing.

"That doesn't change my answer." He jabbed the pitchfork into a bale of hay to separate the sections. "Which is no, in case there was any doubt."

Jack snarled. "Without your help, the pack will die."

"Then so be it." He tossed a couple of hay leaves into the donkey stall before turning back to the wargs. "I have no reason to save it. None of you have ever treated me as anything other than an insect. I'm not even sure why you never killed me."

"Because of your parents, you idiot," Jack said. Tracker didn't know much about diplomacy, but he did know it wasn't wise to insult the person you were asking help from. "They didn't want you dead."

Tracker snorted. "They just wanted me enslaved. Tortured."

"They loved you."

"*Bullfuckingshit*," he roared, suddenly furious at their lies, their insults, their fucking *arrogance* in thinking he'd ever, in a million years, help them do anything except jump off a cliff. "My mother wouldn't even look in my direction! My father beat me so badly once that my master refused to let me go back to the pack for a moon run for three years." Not that he'd wanted to go. But some instincts were hard to deny. "So don't give me this load of crap about how much they loved me."

"Tracker?" There was a light tap at the barn door, and Stacey stepped inside. "Um…I heard you yelling. I didn't realize you had…guests."

Tracker gestured to the door with the pitchfork. "They were just leaving."

After a slight pause and a good look at the pitchfork, Lud inclined his head. "This isn't over, slave. We won't let our pack die. And we will do anything, and I mean *anything*, to keep that from happening."

They filed out, but on the way through the door, Lud and Jack both gave Stacey threatening glances, and Tracker's gut tightened. He wouldn't put it past the assholes to hurt her in order to get what they wanted.

To her credit, she lifted her chin and met their gazes with a hard one of her own, daring them to touch her.

He loved that she had the heart of a warrior.

"What was that about?" she asked after they'd gone.

"Nothing."

"Yeah?" She jammed her fists on her hips. "It sure didn't look like nothing."

"It's nothing," he repeated. "They want my help, but they're not going to get it."

"Help with what?"

"What does it matter?" He gripped the pitchfork so hard he was surprised the wood didn't snap under pressure. "Why do you even care?"

Her lids flew up in surprise, and her cheeks, pink from the cold, went even pinker. "Because I care about you, you big dope. And Jillian cares about you. Don't you think she'd be concerned if she were the one who had walked in on that conversation instead of me?"

"Are you going to tell her?"

"Only if you don't."

"Dammit, Stacey—"

"Dammit, what?" She threw up her hands in an angry gesture. He hated that she was so cute when she was pissed. Made it hard for a guy to hold onto his self-righteous pity party. "You're upset because people care about you?"

"No one cares about me," he shot back, managing to still feel sorry for himself despite her cuteness. "No one has ever cared about me."

"That's not true and you know it. Harvester cared enough about you to give you to Jillian. She wanted you to have a good life. She could have sold you to some scumbag, but she didn't. And Jillian and Reseph care a lot about you. I care. And I don't know what the pack thing was about—"

"It wasn't about caring, I can promise you that."

"Then what was it about?"

"They came to tell me that my parents and all my siblings are dead."

She slapped her hand over her mouth. "Oh, God. I'm so sorry."

Tracker shrugged and went back to forking hay into the stalls. "Shit happens."

"*Shit happens*?" Stacey stormed over and took the pitchfork from him. "Tracker, what the hell? I get that your family sold you into slavery, but you can open up to me about what their deaths mean. I don't buy that your pack jerks came all this way for the announcement. Tell me the truth."

Wordlessly, he yanked the pitchfork away from her, and Stacey huffed.

"Last night we were hot and heavy on the couch, and now you're acting like I'm a monster."

"You're not a monster," he said. "You're just—"

"Just what?"

"You're just like everyone else."

* * * *

Just like everyone else?

Stacey stared at Tracker, baffled by his behavior. Obviously, he was still pissed about last night. More so, it seemed.

"What does that mean, I'm like everyone else?"

"I heard you talking to Jillian. She said she didn't want me. You said you didn't either."

She thought back on the conversation and cringed when she realized how bad it must have sounded to him. "We didn't mean that we didn't want *you*. We meant we didn't want you as a *slave*." She paused to gather her thoughts. "I know I haven't handled your situation well," she admitted. "Your world is so strange. All the despicable rules and violence that's normal to you goes against everything I am as a human, and I tend to be kind of blunt in my opinions." It didn't help that she'd been bombarded by absolutely appalling information in the DART manuals lately. "So no, I couldn't deal with owning someone. The very idea horrifies me. But I *do* want you, Tracker. And Jillian gave us her blessing. For real," she added, when he gave her a skeptical glance. "She even sent you a text with explicit permission."

For some reason, that didn't seem to make him feel any better, and he threw down the pitchfork with a curse. "How do you want me? Sex? Is that it? Because I don't think you know what you're getting into. I'm a werewolf, Stacey. Violent and abnormal. I'm not a tame human like you're used to."

"Trust me," she muttered. "I've never thought of you as tame."

"So you think you can handle me? You think you can deal with what I have to offer?" He laughed bitterly. "I have nothing to offer. I have, literally, nothing." He made an encompassing gesture around the barn. "None of this is mine. Not the barn, not the land, not even my cabin." He pinched the collar of his sweatshirt. "Not even the clothes on my body belong to me. Real fucking sexy, isn't it?"

"You do have a lot to offer, Tracker. You have you."

He barked out another laugh. "Yeah, me. I'm a great catch."

"You're sweet. You're strong. You're smart. I've been watching you for years, and I've seen you tend to hurt animals. I watched you feed and care for two orphaned lambs that no one thought would live. You're a good, decent person, and Jillian will allow you to be anything you want.

If you want more than this, I'll help you."

"I can't want more, Stacey! Don't you see? I'm bound by my slave bond. I'm not allowed to own anything. I'm not allowed to have a mate. Hell, I'm not even allowed to think on my own. My entire *existence* belongs to my master."

She couldn't imagine living like that, but she also knew that Jillian would allow him all those things and more.

"Tracker, Jillian will allow you to have a mate, and property, and a job if you want. She's tried to tell you that a million times. You're the one who is refusing to accept it."

He yanked open the side door to let the animals in from their outside yard. "You don't understand. Jillian doesn't understand. None of that is up to her. It's part of the slave agreement, and masters are bound to it just like I am. They can't allow me to have a mate or to own property. If I break the rules, my master is obligated to punish me. If *they* break the rules, I will be taken away. It's so fucked up. They're allowed to kill us, but they can't let us have any kind of freedom or happiness."

She swallowed. Hard. Every time she thought she had a handle on what his bond involved, there was more. And it kept getting worse. "Oh my God."

"Somehow," he said wryly, "I don't think God has anything to do with it."

She had no doubt about that. Slavery was evil, plain and simple, whether demons engaged in it or humans did.

The animals filed in, nudging her with their noses as they ran past, eager to get to their food. Tracker closed the stall doors, but as the last latch clicked into place, he remained, his fists resting on the top of the gate, his head bowed, his thick arms bearing a lot more weight than just his muscle and bone.

"Stacey..." His voice echoed through the barn, low, rough, and pained. "I can't have anything. But if I could..."

Her breath caught, and she found herself moving closer to him, her boots barely making a sound on the straw-strewn floor.

"What?" she whispered. "What would you want?"

His big body shuddered, and then, like a force of fucking nature that sucked all the oxygen out of the barn, he swung around and his gaze drilled into her. Went dark. Smoky.

Feral.

"You," he said. "I can't take a mate, but I want you."

Chapter 12

Tracker couldn't believe he'd just said that. It was the boldest thing he'd ever said, and the fact that he felt comfortable saying it was yet another way he'd changed since his bond had transferred to Jillian.

Stacey stood there, eyes shot wide, her mouth falling open. Her body language said she was shocked, maybe appalled, and if he weren't a werewolf, he'd be alarmed by her reaction.

But her scent…her scent told a different story.

She was turned on.

Wildly turned on.

They stood there, staring at each other as if wondering who would make the first move. He'd never made any move before. Ever, in his entire life. But he was strung out, stressed by the appearance of his pack members, and riding the fever that came with the approaching full moon. He'd never thought a moment like this would come, and dammit, he was going to take advantage of it.

Even if he was punished for what he was about to do, even if he was put to death for it, it would be the highlight of his life.

He closed the distance between them in half a dozen strides. He didn't think, simply let instinct take over as he gripped her shoulders, took her mouth, and pushed her against the barn wall.

She kissed him back, fiercely, as if she was as starved for this as he was. And fisted his shirt in both hands, holding him against her.

As if he was going anywhere.

Propping his forearm against the wood wall, he thrust his fingers into her silky hair, gripping her waist with his other hand, forcing her even closer. Her moan of appreciation rose from deep in her chest, making her breasts vibrate against him.

It was cold outside, chilly in the barn, but the heat sparking between them threatened to burn it all down. Then she lifted one leg and hooked her calf around his, and the friction of her jeans rubbing his cock through his own pants made him moan too.

"You are so freaking hot," Stacey murmured against his mouth, and then she rolled her hips in a searingly sexual motion that damned near had him ripping off her clothes with his teeth.

Settle down.

He told himself that over and over, even as he mentally pinched himself to make sure this was real. He had never allowed himself to hope, or even dream, that something like this could happen. Not once in his entire life. There was no point. He'd never talked to a single fellow slave who had known anyone who'd been set free.

The only freedom a slave got was in death. It was the best someone like him could hope for.

Now he was as free as he could possibly be while still being bonded to a master, and he was with a female. And not just any female. Stacey was awesome. She was generous. Brave. Strong. Funny. She'd made his whole world brighter. He hadn't known how lonely he was until the night he'd carried her through his doorway.

Fuck Death. He *was* free now.

A growl ripped from his throat as he repositioned his mouth at her neck and bit down. Just a nip, enough to make her suck air and then quiver with pleasure. He nipped again, lightly, along her collar bone, and she dropped her hands and shoved them beneath his shirt. Her palms rode up his abs, so gently that he hissed in shock when she embedded her nails into his chest.

She was magnificent.

This time when he bit her, it wasn't a nip. He sank his teeth into the soft spot between her shoulder and neck, and lightly, so as not to break her delicate skin but enough to hold her, he clamped his jaw.

The most beautiful, rough, sexy sound came from her, and suddenly her hands were at his fly, tearing at the buttons until he could feel the cool air hit his hard cock through the thin fabric of his boxer briefs.

"I didn't take you for an underwear guy," she breathed as she trailed her fingers along his shaft.

He broke the bite and licked the spot he'd bitten. "Reseph said chicks like them."

"Mmm-hmm. We do. But right now, they need to go."

She tugged the waistband down to free his cock and when her fist curled around it, he bit his cheek to keep from embarrassing himself.

"Stacey," he gasped, and he felt her smile against his cheek.

"I can't wait," she said. "I want you."

She had no idea how badly he'd needed to hear that. But not like this. Not in the barn like an animal.

Not that doing her like an animal sounded like a bad thing to him. But she was human, and so was Jillian, who would probably not appreciate what he did to her best friend.

"We…we should go inside—"

She squeezed his shaft, shutting him up. "Absolutely not. Not now. Later. I can't wait that long."

If she kept doing that, they'd be at the point of no return in about five seconds.

Her hand slid up and cupped the tip.

Four seconds.

Gripping tightly, she jacked her hand down, up, down again.

Three seconds.

Her fingers tickled his sac.

Two.

Fuuuuck…stop! Lifting her roughly, he placed her, shoulder high, on a pile of hay bales.

"I need to see you." He tugged on her pants, yanking them and her underwear down to her thighs. "*Taste* you."

"Oh, I do like the sound of that," she whispered as she arched her body to help him remove her pants.

Which left her open to him, her creamy thighs spread, her glistening sex waiting.

And she wasn't shy about it, her gray eyes drilling into him as she leaned back on her elbows.

"I need a distraction," she cajoled. "The hay is kinda pokey."

As much as he wanted to scale the hay mountain and mount her, there were other things he wanted more. His mouth watered as he stepped between her legs and positioned them over his shoulders. She was inches from him now, her sexual perfume driving him crazy as he kissed the tender flesh of her inner thighs.

He took his time working his way inward, peppering her skin with kisses and flirty licks until she was squirming, trying to angle her body against his hungry mouth. He didn't want to tell her how he'd learned to do this, but he was good at it, and he knew it.

But this would be the first time he wanted to drag it out.

He teased her, lapping at her with the flat of his tongue, never parting her folds or tasting her sensitive inner flesh. She watched him, her lower lip trapped by her teeth as she whimpered with need. Holding her gaze, he rimmed her opening and dipped two fingers inside. She cried out, clenching hard around his knuckles.

Her head fell back as she rocked her hips, fucking his hand as he flicked his tongue over her clit, just barely, teasing her more. Her heady scent hit him like an aphrodisiac, making his cock throb with impatience.

Another first.

He couldn't wait to get inside her. Couldn't wait to feel her slick heat around his shaft, her muscles rippling along its length.

But not until he'd made her come at least twice with his mouth.

"T-Tracker, oh, I'm…"

Not yet.

He withdrew his fingers and waited a few breaths before replacing them with his tongue.

"No," she breathed, "harder."

He slowed it down, torturing her in the best way. Shallow licks, deep penetrations, and all so, so lazy.

"Please, Tracker," she moaned, her female need triggering his male instinct to fulfill it.

He stopped teasing and kissed her deep. His tongue swirled around her swollen nub until she started bucking, her breathing shallow, and then he sucked her there.

"Yesssss!"

In the background, he heard one of the goats bleat in alarm, but he focused on Stacey and her shouts of pleasure that went on and on. He eased her down, but before she caught her breath, he licked again, lower, harder, pressing into that sensitive, swollen place.

Stacey cried out again, her voice hoarser than it was before. But before she'd even finished, she reached down and tugged at his hair, encouraging him to climb up the hay bales so he was kissing her, his cock probing her entrance.

He thrust inside her with no finesse, no teasing, no Nice To Meet You. He inhaled her gasp at his invasion, and then he started pumping, his body taking control of the show as his brain shut down for the ride.

Her nails scored his back as she rocked with him, bringing them both into a place where nothing mattered. There was no past, no future, just two souls connecting. He'd never felt like this. This…whole.

His pace turned frenzied as the pleasure shot higher, became electric. He came in a firestorm of pleasure, shouting into the rafters.

She joined him, and he kept going until they were wrung out, spent, draped over the hay bales like melted marshmallows.

It seemed like a year before she arched beneath him to kiss his neck and murmur, "I say we take this to the bedroom. Less hay. Fewer clothes. Soft mattress."

He pushed to his elbows and looked down at her, into drowsy, sexed-up eyes. "You want more?"

"Mmm." She smiled and sighed. "I have a feeling that with you, it'll never be enough."

Funny, he felt the same about her.

* * * *

Whenever Stacey fell off her horse as a child, her dad would tell her to climb right back on.

She thought about that as she fell off Tracker, landing in an exhausted flop on the mattress. Because she'd just ridden him for, like, miles, and there was no way she was getting back in the saddle.

For at least half an hour.

Her breath came in fits, raspy, painful fits as she lay there, spread-eagled on her back, one arm hanging off the bed, one lying across his chest, but she wouldn't have it any other way.

That was the best sex she'd ever had.

"Tonight," she rasped, "you're not sleeping on the couch."

"I wasn't planning on it."

She shivered at the masculine possession in his voice. Shivered, but didn't move. And when he trailed the backs of his fingers along the underside of her arm in long, languid strokes, she went completely liquid. She was never moving again.

Night had fallen at some point, leaving them engulfed in darkness and surrounded by silence broken only by the sound of their labored breathing.

"I lost count of my orgasms." She swallowed dryly, wishing she'd had the foresight to bring a glass of water to bed. But they'd been in such a hurry, kissing their way across the floor, leaving a trail of clothes and hay as they went.

"Three in the barn," he said. "And three in the bedroom."

She laughed at the fact that he'd not only counted but had taken her words so literally.

She hadn't lost count at all, and he'd missed one. She'd had four in the barn.

"So," she said, losing herself in the tingles his touch left on her skin. "Tell me something about you that I don't know."

"Why?"

"Pillow talk. It's something people do after sex."

"Oh." She felt him tense, and she was about to tell him he didn't have to talk if he didn't want to when he took a deep breath. "I don't have to chain myself up on nights of the full moon, but I do."

She turned her head to look at him, but she could barely make out his features. "Why don't you have to chain yourself?"

"I'm *Pricolici*. I was born a werewolf, so I can control myself after the shift. I'm not a danger to humans."

She'd read that born werewolves could control themselves much better than those who were turned, but she hadn't known how far that increased sense of self-awareness extended. "Then why would you chain yourself?"

"Because my pack instinct is strong." He sounded annoyed by that. "When I shift, I crave companionship, even if my pack mates are assholes."

She sagged into the mattress so far her spine felt like it hit the floor. He must be so lonely. "What if I were to sit with you? Next time you shift?"

"You would do that?" Before she could answer, he shook his head. "No. I said I'm not a danger to humans, but with you…"

"With me, what?"

Silence stretched. Finally, a growled, "But with you I might be."

"You wouldn't hurt me. I know that." Before he started some bullshit "I must wrap you in bubble wrap and protect you from All Things Bad and Evil" routine she'd seen Reseph pull on Jillian, she reached over and put her finger to his lips. "Shh. We'll talk about it later."

She *would* get her way, and she *would* keep him company.

"Now it's your turn," she said, hoping he'd ignore the quick change of subject. "You ask me a question."

"You said you kissed a lot of humans. How many?"

"Oh," she rasped, wishing she had that water, "you're getting right to it. Just whipped that out. Okay." This wasn't going to be awkward at all. She turned over so she was facing him, propped up on her elbow. "I had my first date in high school. I've dated a lot of guys since, but most were pretty casual. You know, a few dinners, a movie, and then you kinda figure out you're not going anywhere because he has a gambling problem or a stalker ex or he constantly talks like a radio DJ." Ugh, that had been so bizarre. Kevin was always narrating shit in a DJ voice. As if hearing him read a restaurant menu like it was a commercial was so sexy. "But I dated a couple that I really liked, and we were together for a year or so."

"Where are they now?"

"Most are still around, in town, or at least in the state. I hardly ever see them." She slid her palm up his arm, mapping his ropey muscles and hard veins beneath his smooth skin. "My turn. I need to know about your skin care routine." She leaned over and kissed his shoulder, letting her lips linger as she inhaled the mingled scents of hay, pine, and man. "It's so soft."

"It's part of the slave bond. Masters like clean, smooth flesh to wreck, so after we're hurt, we heal almost as good as new within a couple of days. Same with our minds. They do something to our brains so we recover from mental trauma quickly." He trailed his fingers over the sensitive skin of her wrist. "Can't have your slaves getting angry about their circumstances or going stark-raving mad or drooling in a corner, you know?"

"No words," she spat. "There are no words for that kind of cruelty." She wanted just five minutes with any one of his past masters. And with the slavers. What sick, demented fucks. "They took everything from you, even your damned *scars*."

"No, the scars are still there," he said, so casually it was worse than if he'd been upset. "Most can't see them."

"Most?"

"Once, Eidolon's mate, Tayla, was here. She saw me, and she didn't say anything, but I saw her reaction. She's part Soulshredder. She can see scars others can't. Emotional ones too. I probably looked like a mass of walking hamburger to her."

Good…god. Stacey held him tight as he revealed more about his past. The things he'd lived through and that had been done to him left her an emotional mess. She went through a dozen tissues before he realized how much he'd shared and shut down. But she was grateful for every word. She might be haunted by the things he told her, but if it lessened his pain, she would bear it for him.

"Tracker?" She leaned over and kissed him. "Your life sucked."

He laughed and rolled her over, driving his thigh between her legs. "It did. But it's getting better every day."

Chapter 13

Stacey yawned, stretching out in bed like a big, satiated cat before squirming over to cuddle with Tracker. So she was disappointed to find that his side of the bed was cold.

Beyond the closed bedroom door, the sound of the front door opening and squeaking shut was a muffled thud. Heavy footsteps crossed the wood floor, coming closer.

Tracker opened the bedroom door quietly, but he didn't need to.

"It's okay," she said on another yawn. "I'm awake. What's up?"

"The road is cleared. I'm going into town for supplies. Do you want me to take you home?"

Home? Hell, no, she didn't want to go. She'd loved her time here with Tracker. It had been a welcome break from real life and the real world, and she didn't want it to end.

She did have to report her accident to the police and the insurance company, and she had to contact her supervisor at DART. But she could do that from here with the new phone Jillian had given her.

"Nope," she said. "I can stay a little longer. If that's okay."

He crossed the room in a blur and kissed her long and hard, making heat ripple between her legs for about the millionth time in twelve hours. She was about to grab him by the coat lapels and tumble him into bed when he pulled back.

"It's definitely okay." He traced a fingertip along her jaw in a gentle, loving gesture that made her belly flutter. "But…"

Uh-oh. She sat up in alarm. "But what?"

"Tonight is the full moon."

"Oh, right." Relieved that it wasn't something horrible, she flopped back down on the pillow. "You need to lock yourself up."

And she'd be there to keep him company. He just didn't know it yet.

"Not this time." His voice was a resonant, serrated growl brimming with restrained anger. "I'm going to visit my pack."

She did *not* like the sound of that. He mentioned that he needed to find out why they'd been lurking around, but it hadn't occurred to her that he would have to leave to do it. "Why can't you just call?"

He scrubbed his hand over his face. "Not for this. I need to make it clear that they aren't getting what they want from me."

She sat up again. Her abs were getting a workout. "What do they want?"

"Something I can't give them."

Tracker was the tightest-lipped, most private person she'd ever encountered. She was starting to understand why he kept everything to himself, but she wanted him to learn to trust her.

His fucking slave masters couldn't control *that.*

So, she pressed, because she remembered that some of the things he couldn't have as a slave were property, freedom, and a mate.

"You said your parents were dead, so if your people want something from you…did you inherit property?"

"Not exactly."

"Then what?"

Shaking his head, he swiped his keys off the dresser. "This isn't the time to talk about it."

"Then when will be?" She swung her feet over the edge of the bed, prepared to block the doorway if she had to. "I get that you've had a lot to deal with in your life, and I won't force you to talk about your past until you're ready. But this is current, and if it's something I can help you with, I want to do that."

"You can't."

So infuriating. "How do you know?"

His gaze fell to her bare legs, following them up to where the oversized T-shirt she'd borrowed from him barely covered places he'd gotten real intimate with last night. Heat pooled there as she remembered the feel of his lips, his tongue, and she casually shifted to make the shirt bunch a little higher, giving him a better view.

Hey, she wasn't above using sex to get what she wanted.

Mainly because it was sex she wanted. The pillow talk would get her the information afterward. He'd opened up so much last night.

His gaze snapped up as if he'd suddenly figured out her ploy. "They want me to take a mate."

She choked a little, and the hot curl of desire froze solid. Surely he hadn't said what she thought he'd said. "A…mate? Like, a wife?"

"It's a little different for werewolves, especially born weres like myself, but yeah."

"I don't understand." She was going to hyperventilate. "Don't they know you can't?"

"I don't think they care." He whipped off his black stocking cap and shoved his fingers through his hair. "They might have worked something out with the slaver guild, which is why I need to talk to them."

She resisted the urge to tell him to call Jillian. He wouldn't, and this might be another one of those things she "didn't understand." But that didn't mean she was going to keep her opinion to herself. She'd never been good at that.

"I don't like it. Stay here. Lock yourself up."

"I can't." He tugged the cap back on. "This won't go away."

"What'll they do when you refuse?"

"They won't kill me, if that's what you're worried about. The pack's very existence depends on me being alive."

That didn't make any sense, but she was too focused on the fact that they wanted him to be with another female to think too hard on it. "I still don't like it."

"I don't either." His chest rose and fell in a couple of powerful breaths, as if he was considering exactly how much he didn't like it. "I'll explain everything when I get back from town. Is there anything you need?"

"Ooh, yes." She welcomed the change of subject *and* the fact that he was actually willing to talk about it later. Progress! Maybe there was hope for him, yet. "Will you pick up some pork chops? There's a recipe in one of Suzanne's books I wanted to try but we didn't have all the ingredients. We'll need cream too. And mushrooms. We can do dinner before you go all beastie."

"You got it. I'll be back soon."

She listened to the sound of the truck starting up and driving off, and then snuggled into the covers for a little while longer. It wasn't until the sun started peeking through the breaks in the curtains that she finally crawled out of bed and showered.

Today would be the last day she'd have to wear Jillian's borrowed clothes. As excited as she was to have her own wardrobe available again, it meant she'd be alone in her house.

She'd only been with Tracker for a few days, but it was enough to know she wanted to be with him more. She'd spent an entire year basically living with one guy, Joel, and she'd never felt as close to him as she did to Tracker in a much shorter time.

So she might not be forced to stay with him any longer, but that didn't mean she was going to stop seeing him. His cabin was only about twenty minutes from her rented house on the outskirts of town, so they could work it out.

Assuming he wasn't forced to take a mate.

What the hell? It couldn't happen. He said so himself. But what if he was right and the werewolves had worked out a deal with the slavers?

Tracker wouldn't call Jillian about this, but Stacey could. She eyed the new iPhone, but as she reached for it, her hand shook. To tell Jillian about this would be a massive betrayal to Tracker. But to not tell Jillian would be a massive betrayal to *her*.

Son of a bitch.

Torn between loyalties, she turned away from the phone and did a little stress cleaning while she contemplated her next move.

And who she was going to betray.

Tracker kept a spotless house, so there wasn't much to tidy up. When she ran out of stuff to clean after like, five minutes, she went out to the barn to visit the animals. Maybe they'd have some advice for her.

She'd known the critters for years. She'd even gone with Jillian to pick up the donkeys from a neglect situation in Wyoming. Surely they could give her some comfort. In the very least, they could listen as she talked out loud to herself.

She flung open the door with a grin. "Hey, guys. It's your Aunt Stacey! Hope you've gotten over the trauma of what Tracker and I did in front of you last night..."

She trailed off at the sight of the two huge dudes who had been here yesterday, standing at the goat stall, one with a rope looped around Rick's neck.

They stared at her, obviously as surprised as she was.

Shit. She had no weapons, and as competent as she was with hand-to-hand combat, she doubted she could overpower two werewolves who looked like they might know something about fighting.

Think. Be smart. Casual.

One of the lessons she'd learned from years in law enforcement and more recently as an agent for DART was to de-escalate whenever possible, and this seemed to be a situation made for exactly that.

"So, I'm just going to go back in the house and let Tracker know you're here. He was putting on his jacket when I walked out, so he'll be outside in a minute. Oh, and release the goat."

As calmly as she could and hoping they bought her lie about Tracker, she closed the door and headed toward the safety of the house…and her cell phone.

She started running the moment she heard the barn door wrench open, but before she'd made it a dozen feet, something hit her so hard she flew into the air and landed in a heap in the snow.

A heavy body came down on top of her with a ferocious snarl.

"Not so fast, little human." Hot, fetid breath engulfed her face and nearly made her gag. "We know Tracker isn't here."

She gasped as he wrenched her arms behind her back and hauled her to her feet.

The other male, the big white-haired bastard, came up to her and sniffed her, a long, gross inhale. "Tracker's bitch," he rumbled.

"She could be useful," the other one said. "Better than the goat."

The blond nodded. "We'll eat the goat. The female will be our leverage."

"Leverage?" She stomped on her captor's foot, and he cuffed her on the side of the head. "Ouch! Leverage for what? And I swear, if you so much as touch that goat—"

"You'll what, *human*?"

She lifted her chin and glared in defiance. "I have very powerful friends."

"I'm sure you do."

Before she could tell them exactly how powerful, the asshole in front of her cocked back his meaty fist, and then her world became nothing but pain followed by darkness.

* * * *

Tracker couldn't remember a time when he'd been in such a hurry to get back home.

Home. This was also the first time he truly allowed himself to think of his cabin in that way.

Always before, he'd simply resided wherever his current owner kept him. He'd never actually had a home. And even though Jillian had given him a place to live in safety and comfort, his little cabin had still felt temporary. Or like a dog house for the family pet.

But Stacey had made it feel like a home, and he couldn't wait to get back to it.

Yes, she'd have to leave at some point for her own place, and he had business with his pack. But he was hoping that afterward, they could be together. Even if the slave contract didn't allow for a real, official mate, they could still have a relationship.

Assuming, of course, she wanted one.

He didn't let doubt creep in though, because nothing was going to ruin his great mood.

He turned onto the driveway and drove down the packed snow, taking a detour to back up to the barn. He had a truck full of feed for the goats and donkeys and wood for patching the roof, so he'd go ahead and unload before going into the cabin with the groceries.

He couldn't wait for tonight's cooking lesson. One of the things he'd done when he woke up this morning was to read the cookbook, practicing words and looking up definitions.

He had no idea what an artichoke tasted like, but one of the recipes called for their hearts, so he'd purchased two at the store.

They were weird. And pokey. And they looked poisonous, like the bile bulbs in Sheoul. Still, he figured humans wouldn't sell lethal things as food, so he'd popped them in a bag and hoped Stacey would help him prepare them. If she didn't know how, there was always Google.

He caught himself whistling as he backed the truck up to the barn door, although he couldn't name the tune. Something Stacey had taught him to dance to, he thought.

Maybe they could have another lesson tonight before his shift. Well, they could try. He had a feeling that he wouldn't make it for five minutes, pressed up against her body, before he tore off her clothes with his teeth.

An erotic purr rattled his chest as he bailed out of the truck. Screw waiting until after dinner to get her naked. He was going to make it happen as soon as he was done with this.

Working quickly, he heaved the barn door open, flipped the truck's tailgate down, and threw a bag of feed over his shoulder.

"Sorry guys, but I'm not lingering today—"

He froze, mid-step, just inside the threshold.

Something was wrong. The donkeys were unusually talkative, and the goats were unusually quiet. Hackles raised, he looked inside the goat stall.

Evie looked at him with wild eyes and gave him a pitiful bleat. Rick was missing.

He dropped the bag of food onto a bale of hay. It landed with an ominous thud.

"Rick?" Silence greeted him, as he knew it would. The goat couldn't have gotten out of the stall on his own.

Maybe Stacey had him out for some reason.

Shit.

Breathe. It's probably nothing.

He threw open the smaller access door that faced his cabin. The chilly air slapped him across the face, but it was the footprints that punched him in the gut.

Stacey's size eight feet. One tiny set of goat hooves.

And two huge sets of boots that didn't belong to Tracker.

With a vile Sheoulic curse, he sprinted toward the cabin, following Stacey's tracks. She'd walked to the barn. Then started to walk back.

Then, about halfway to safety, she'd broken into a run.

A few feet later, she went down. The snow was churned up in what must have been a violent struggle.

There was blood.

"Stacey!" he screamed as he tore off to the cabin. He knew he wouldn't find her there, but he had to look. He had to be sure.

As he feared, she was nowhere to be found.

But he knew where to find her.

With a snarl and another Sheoulic oath, he strapped on the ankle knife sheath Reseph had given him, as well as the pistol and holster the Horseman had taught him to use. He didn't have a supply of silver bullets, but regular bullets would cause enough damage to get Tracker out of a dangerous situation.

He knew Reseph and his brothers were busy, but if Jillian could send Limos, she'd be a powerfully ally. Quickly, he dialed, but Jillian didn't answer. Which meant she was either sleeping or flying.

He was going to have to go at this alone.

Good thing he was used to that.

In his bedroom, he hesitated at the dresser.

The coin Harvester had given him years ago glinted from its resting place between two knots in the wood finish. He'd tossed it there the day she'd given it to him, and he hadn't touched it since. It was slightly askew, probably Stacey's doing, and he resisted the urge to nudge it back in place and leave it there.

Harvester told him that if he ever needed her, the coin would summon her. He'd sworn he'd never use it. If he never saw her again, that would be great.

But Stacey's life was at stake, so he pocketed it. For her, he would do anything.

Even summon his former master.

Chapter 14

The world was on fire.

It must be for Stacey to be in this much pain.

She moaned, the vibration antagonizing the ache in her chest. Spasms made every breath feel like flame. And her face throbbed. Actually, her entire body throbbed. And if both arms were out of socket, it would explain a lot.

Shivering despite the sizzling pain, she sat up, blinking as she tried to stay upright. Dust motes floated in slices of light that blinded her until she scooted back into the shadows cast by slats of wood. What time was it? Judging by the change in the lay of the shadows, it was a couple of hours later than the first time she'd woken to find herself on a filthy burlap sack. In a freezing, drafty shack full of old logging and trapping equipment. Giant, rusty saw blades had been propped against the walls or hung from hooks, and wicked-looking leg traps dangled from the rafters. Bits of fur still clung to the tarnished metal teeth.

Who the hell owned this shed? She'd seen enough horror movies to be *really* freaked out. She might come out the hero in those Would You Survive a Horror Movie quizzes online, but in real life she was potentially the *character who just had sex and now must die.*

Well, fuck that. She might die, but she wasn't going to make it easy for them.

Groaning, she shoved to her feet, hoping she'd stay upright for more than thirty seconds this time. Her attempt to stand earlier had been a colossal failure involving the spins, vomit, and blacking out.

She was no medical expert, but she was pretty sure she had a concussion.

She made it to her feet out of sheer stubbornness. She couldn't stop the swaying, though, and had to reach out to catch herself on a rickety sawhorse.

Okay. Breathe. You can do this.

Swallowing her nausea, she shuffled carefully around the little shed, taking a lay of the land, looking for possible means of escape or anything that could be used as a weapon.

One would think that in a shack full of pointy blades and wicked traps, there'd be something useful, but nope. The saw blades were made for heavy equipment, multiple humans, or The Hulk. The leg traps had skull-crushing potential if swung by their chains, but she'd rather have the speed and multiple uses of a blade if she could find one.

Unfortunately, no one had been thoughtful enough to leave a nice sharp dagger or machete lying around.

Resigned, she eased one of the smaller traps off its wall hook and lowered it to the ground as quietly as she could. No sense in alerting any guard outside that she was contemplating murder.

She hauled it by the chain, limping and lurching like a zombie over to the door. Still being as silent as rattling metal allowed, she concealed it under a rusty old bucket. As she straightened, voices rang out, distant, but growing closer.

Stacey backed up, a surge of adrenaline washing away all her pain. A shadow rippled along the boards, and between the slats, flashes of someone in jeans and a red jacket. The sound of clicking locks made her jump, and a moment later, the door swung open with a grating creak.

A burly dude dressed in black took a stance outside, and a tall, slender woman entered, her long red hair fanned out over the fur-lined hood of her winter coat. "I brought you food."

Okay, so the plan wasn't to kill her right away.

The woman placed a thermos and a paper bag on the rickety sawhorse opposite the bucket. "There's hot stew, and a biscuit and spoon in the bag." She tucked her gloved hands into her parka and regarded Stacey with an almost bored gaze, so sure that she wasn't a threat. "What's your name?"

"Fuck you." Stacey widened her stance, ready to beat this chick's ass. And also to make herself steadier on her feet. "Who are you? Why are you doing this?"

One severely plucked eyebrow climbed up a fraction of an inch, as if this had just gotten marginally more interesting. "Tracker didn't tell you?"

"Tell me what? That some crazy werewolves were going to kidnap me?"

The bored lady shrugged. "We only wanted the goat. You got in the way."

The thermos.

Stacey gasped in horror at the shiny gray cylinder. "You—"

Bored Lady laughed. "We wanted the goat as leverage. That's a roast from Yukon Dave's Grocery. But now that we have you as a bargaining chip, the goat is for tomorrow night."

"A bargaining chip?" Stacey mentally calculated how fast she could cross the floor between them. "For what?"

"We need him to give us a child."

So this was definitely Tracker's pack. These were the assholes who had given him up into a life of hell and now expected him to come when they called?

Also...*a child*? He'd failed to mention that little tidbit of information. He'd only talked about a mate. If she survived this, she was so going to ream him a new one.

"You people are insane." She did another round of calculations and concluded with certainty that she'd never get across the floor in time to take this chick by surprise. She wouldn't even get close. Even if Stacey somehow succeeded, Bored Lady was a werewolf with superpowers, and there was the werewolf guard outside to deal with. "He'll never agree." God, she sounded like the captured love interest of a blackmailed superhero.

Problem was, this was probably a horror flick, not a superhero movie with a happy ending.

"Oh, he will. If he ever wants to see you alive again, he will, and he'll do it tonight." She stepped outside, but before she slammed the door closed, she added, "Or you'll take the place of the goat."

* * * *

Tracker stepped out of the Harrowgate, prepared for an ambush. But as he stood there, tense and ready for action, the only things moving in the remote Canadian wilderness were birds.

Which meant the pack wasn't going to antagonize him any more than they already had. At least, not yet. He had a feeling things were going to get real damned antagonistic very soon.

Tucking his blade away, he started trudging the half mile to pack headquarters, which was basically a village outside of a larger human community where pack members worked and pretended to be functioning members of society.

And in a way, many were. His pack origins were in Hungary, but they'd moved dozens of times over the last century, trying to stay one step ahead of The Aegis and other various enemies, including other werewolf packs. They'd evolved, too, as younger members who were less homo sapien-phobic intertwined their lives with their human coworkers and neighbors.

Still, as Tracker had learned over the years, the New and Improved pack was still pretty damned vicious, and his parents had ruled it with iron claws.

The hike was easy in only about six inches of snow, and he wondered how the hell Colorado had gotten three feet of the shit recently, but the storm had somehow missed these assholes. It was sunny, the temperature above freezing, and he was sweating by the time he approached the small, gated community.

They were waiting for him.

The second he strode through the gate, he was flanked by two big, blond, bearded males named Vandal and Andris.

"We've been expecting you," Vandal said.

"No shit." Tracker pegged them both with hard stares. "You took my master's goat and my female. It was a safe bet I'd come for them."

Andris grinned, flashing all kinds of fang. "Look at you, brother. What happened to the timid whelp you've always been?"

"I'm not your brother," he bit out. "And that timid whelp is gone."

Funny how he only now realized that. So much had changed. Jillian had given him room to grow, and Stacey had given him reason to. He wasn't going back to what he'd been. Not ever.

"It's about fucking time," Andris said. "Between you and me…and Van, I guess, I think you got a shit deal. Your parents were bastards for what they did to you."

Vandal grunted. "They were our leaders. They kept us safe."

"That doesn't mean they were perfect." Andris gave Tracker the side-eye. "Van has always been a fall-in-line guy."

"Fuck off," Vandal muttered.

Andris snorted. "Things will get better with Victoria in charge." He clapped Tracker on the back. "Thanks for helping."

"I'm not here to help. I'm here to take back what's mine."

Van grunted, his beady eyes locked on the path ahead. "You're not getting it until you do what's required."

"We'll work something out," Andris said quickly. He'd always been a peacemaker and one of the few people Tracker didn't despise. "The pack can't run the way it always has. Victoria promised democracy."

"Victoria said what she needed to say to get the human lovers like you to back her," Van said in a voice that made it clear he didn't agree with placating those who sympathized with humans.

Andris took off his Vancouver Canucks hat and scratched his head. "Whatever."

They settled into uncomfortable silence as they guided Tracker toward a cabin near the center of the village. Next door was a tiny church, which had always struck Tracker as odd, given that born werewolves tended to lean more on the demonic side of religion. He supposed the church had simply been there already when they moved here, but if so, why hadn't they torn it down? Maybe they'd converted it into a place of worship for the demon his parents had bargained with to give them the power they'd had. And now that he looked closer, he was certain of that. Aside from the shape of the building, there was no sign that there was anything Christian about it.

When they arrived at the cabin steps, Lud and Jack met them on the porch.

"Glad you decided to show up," Lud said, as if Tracker had a choice. "Victoria is waiting for you inside."

"I'm not going anywhere until I see Stacey."

Lud nodded to Jack, who jogged off, and a moment later, a beeping noise came from Ludwig's pocket. He pulled out his phone and handed it to Tracker.

The sound coming from the phone was staticky as Tracker put it to his ear. "Stacey?"

"Tracker?" Her voice rang out clear as a bell, and his knees nearly collapsed with relief.

"Yeah, it's me." He angled his body away from the crowd of onlookers. He couldn't keep his conversation private, but fuck if he was going to let them see the emotions playing out on his face. "I'm here for you—"

"Don't give them what they want. Don't you dare."

Her fierceness swelled his heart with pride and took his fear for her down a notch. "I need to know you're okay."

"I'm fine, but—"

He didn't hear the rest, because Lud tore the phone from his hands. "That's enough. She's alive and well, and it'll stay that way if you do what you're told."

The cabin door opened, and a svelte redhead came out. Victoria. She looked every inch the queen in black jeans, a long purple and gold blouse that emphasized a trim waist and deep cleavage, and a black scarf draped casually across her shoulders like a mantle of royalty.

She'd clearly already assumed the position of pack leader. Now she needed to make it official.

"Tracker. How nice of you to come."

He wished these assholes would stop making it sound like he was here for a housewarming.

"Come inside," she said in a soft, breathy voice. "I have tea."

"How civilized. Not something I'd expect from people who threatened me and kidnapped an innocent human and defenseless goat."

"We *are* a contradictory bunch," Andris said brightly, and in any other circumstance, Tracker might have liked the guy's sense of humor.

Right now he just wanted to punch him.

Tracker followed Victoria inside the cabin that could have belonged to any human, with its modern tile floors, appliances, and furniture. This had been his parents' place, the nicest house in the village, reserved for the leaders.

He wondered how long his parents had been dead before Victoria had moved in.

Several other pack members greeted him with nods from where they sat in a semicircle around a coffee table laden with plates of cheese and sausage, as well as a teapot and several cups.

Victoria gestured to an empty chair near the blazing fire as Lud and Jack took up sentry positions at the door. "Please, sit."

He was gonna pass on that. "I don't have time for this. Give me my female and my goat. I need to get them back before nightfall."

Cold shadows darkened Victoria's green eyes. "I said, sit."

Tracker folded his arms over his chest and remained where he was.

"Suit yourself," she gritted out. "This will go the same way whether you're sitting or standing." She poured herself a cup of tea and turned to him. "We're going to make some babies, and before you say you're sterile, you should know that your sterility is reversible by the slavers, and they agreed to do that."

"Why would they?"

"Because you are prime breeding stock." She dropped two sugar cubes into her cup. "We promised them all the cubs but one that come from our union. Our kind rarely give birth to a single cub, so if I have more than one, the rest will go to them."

If there was one way to ensure that he would never get her pregnant, that was it. No child of his would *ever* be given into slavery. Still, he held his tongue until he got all the information, such as what was going to happen to Stacey if he refused. He could guess, but he wanted to hear it.

"As a slave, I'm not allowed to take a mate, and that's baked into my bond. It can't be reversed."

Her lips twitched in an amused smile. She was enjoying toying with him like a cat with a mouse. "We won't be mating. Just fucking."

They wouldn't be doing either, but again, he was biding his time. Decades as a slave had taught him a lot about silence and patience. He was one hell of an observer.

For example, he'd noted that at least half of the pack members in attendance had looked uncomfortable when Victoria said they'd give up cubs to slavers.

"And if I refuse?"

"Your female dies."

Man, he wanted to rip her throat out. "I see."

She cocked her head and studied him. "You don't seem particularly bothered."

"Well, honestly, I expected that answer."

"And what is *your* answer?"

"It's a hard no."

"Selfish prick." The leather recliner in the corner creaked as John, a grizzled old guy who'd been with the pack since as long as Tracker could remember, leaned forward. "The pack will die if we don't do this."

Tracker didn't give a shit if the pack died or not, but saying so wouldn't win him any points with any members who might otherwise be tempted to side with him. His best play right now was to stay calm. Reasonable. And not give in to his homicidal urges to slaughter everyone in the room, starting with Victoria.

"As I understand it, my parents gave me up to take control of the pack and protect it from demons." He looked at each member, connecting with them, making them see him and not just a blackmailed breeder. "The demons who were threatening the pack have probably moved on. There's no need to continue giving up infants to the *malibites*."

Victoria shook her head. "Part of the deal they made protected them from assassination within our ranks. Deal came with the stipulation that, if they should die, only someone from their line can take over the pack or every member will wither away within a year."

"Which means we need an heir now," Lud said.

Tracker thought about that. "Make me pack leader. Problem solved." But only until the *malibites* found out. He wasn't allowed any position of power, but Victoria might not know that.

"You?" Victoria laughed. "You know nothing about leading a warg pack. And you already have a job."

"I'll name you regent to rule in my stead. We don't have to have a child."

"We already consulted with the slavers," she responded, dashing his hopes of getting out of here with a lie. "You can't own or be in charge of anything. If you try to enter into a binding agreement like that, your slave bond will alert the slavers, and they will come for you."

Son of a bitch. His patience and desire to remain calm was slipping now. "We have a year to find an acceptable alternative—"

"Enough," she barked. "We're not risking it. I'm entering my breeding heat, so we will do it now or your female will die."

Okay, he was done playing nice. He had one hell of a card to play, and it was time to lay it down.

"My answer is still no, and you *will* accept that."

Victoria arched a thin red eyebrow. "And why would we do that?"

"Because Stacey is my master's best friend. You do *not* want to mess with her."

They all laughed. Victoria nearly spilled her tea. "I'm sure we can handle a silly little human female."

Jillian was a force to be reckoned with, but she wasn't the true threat. They wouldn't know that, though, since he'd never felt the need to tell them. He'd never told them anything, really. "Maybe, but you can't handle her mate."

She rolled her eyes. "We're a powerful pack. I don't care if her mate is a Cruentus demon. We can deal with it."

Tracker paused, savoring the anticipatory silence, which grew more tense the longer he waited. Finally, as people started to squirm, he explained exactly why the entire pack would be fucked if they harmed Stacey.

"My master's mate is no demon. She's married to Pestilence, first Horseman of the Apocalypse." He raised his voice over the gasps and shocked curses. "So unless you want to go through your own personal Armageddon, I suggest you let us all go."

There was a long moment of stunned silence, and then a flurry of panic and yelling until finally Victoria shut them all down.

"Shut up! I need time to think." She gestured to Lud and Jack. "Take him to the stockade. The rest of you, stay here. We have some planning to do."

Chapter 15

Stacey was pretty sure she was going to freeze to death. The hot stew had helped to warm her, but now that she had nothing to do but wait for whatever was to come, the cold had started to seep in.

She rubbed her arms and did laps around the shed, doing her best to devise an escape plan. She kept eyeing the saw blades and traps. Surely there was something she'd missed.

Think outside the box. Think, think, think.

There…one of the saw blades was badly rusted. Maybe she could break off one of the teeth. It wouldn't make much of a weapon, but at this point, she was willing to try anything.

She heaved the thing off the wall and laid it flat on a board, angling it so that a couple of the teeth were hanging off the edge. Praying this would work, she stood on the blade to hold it down while she stomped on the teeth. Nothing. They didn't even bend, let alone break.

Frustrated, she limped over to a small bit of machinery that probably had something to do with lumber or farming or whatever the hell they did here in the middle of nowhere.

The thing was heavy as hell, so maybe if she used it like a bludgeon she'd have better luck breaking the saw blade.

Gathering all her strength and ignoring all her aches and pains, she lifted it as high as she could and dropped it onto the rusted teeth. It bounced off the blade, and oh, joy of joys, one of the teeth was now bent, which would weaken the metal.

Hope gave her a burst of strength, and she struck again. And again. And maybe it was her imagination, but it looked like there was a crack starting about halfway down the tooth. Better for it to break where it connected with the main blade, but she'd take half of a sharp tooth. It might even be easier to conceal between her fingers.

As she struggled to lift the tool again, she heard footsteps approaching.

An injection of fear made her heart race as she eased over to the back side of the shed and put her ear to the wall.

Footsteps came closer, a set from her right and her left, and then they joined up.

A male voice spoke in a hushed whisper. "Did you hear?"

"Hear what?" whispered a female.

"About Tracker?"

"Yeah, no," she said in a snotty voice. "I'm not exactly in the alpha loop."

The voices lowered even more.

"You knew Tracker's master is a human, right?"

"Yeah. So?" the female said, still managing to sound bitter in a whisper.

"She's not just human. She's mated to an underworlder."

"And once again," the female drawled, "I'm going to say, so?"

"Her mate is one of the Four Horsemen of the Apocalypse."

There was a moment of silence, and then a loud, "You're full of shit."

"Shh! I swear. Victoria's all freaked out."

"Shit. So what happens now? Is the pack in danger?"

"I don't know. I overheard Lud saying we might have to hurry up and send Tracker to the slavers so his master can't track us here. It's illegal for a human to own a slave, so they can simply cancel his slave bond with her and she can't track him anymore. We'd be safe then."

"They can do that?"

They moved away from the shack a few feet, and Stacey struggled to hear the next part of the conversation.

"I don't know," the male said. "It's total speculation. But either way, they're discussing getting rid of the evidence."

"Evidence?"

"The goat and Tracker's female."

Stacey's breath clogged in her throat. No one let "evidence" survive.

There was a pause, and then the female squealed in excitement. "A hunt?"

"Yeah. Awesome, huh? How long has it been since we've had a true, old-fashioned full moon human hunt?"

"Decades. Four or five, maybe. I was too young to participate in the last one. That'll be so cool!"

No, not cool. Not cool at all. Holy shit, these monsters were casually discussing how fun it would be to hunt her. Like prey.

The stew in her gut sat there like a vat of toxic waste, threatening to come back up at any moment. Stacey swallowed sickly, over and over, willing it to stay down.

Because now she knew how important it was to have every ounce of energy she could possibly muster.

She was going to have to run for her life.

* * * *

Tracker had fought his captors every step of the way to the old-fashioned stockade near the center of the village. A sign outlining what was probably made-up history had been erected in front of it to keep human visitors from wondering why the hell it was there.

He wondered how his presence, his neck and wrists locked in the wood and metal structure, would be explained. No doubt they'd claim he was an actor, playing a part for tourists.

As if Podunk Village was a coveted destination for those wanting to get away.

And what was extra infuriating was that his trump card hadn't had the effect he was hoping for. He'd figured Victoria would quickly send him, Stacey, and the goat packing after she learned who his master's mate was.

Did she think Reseph would merely sit back and do nothing?

He supposed that assumption wasn't too crazy, given that when the Horseman's evil half, Pestilence, had rampaged across the planet to start the apocalypse, born wargs had sided with him. Maybe Victoria assumed he would owe them for their support. Or that he was still on their side.

They were in for one hell of a surprise, if that was the case. He'd have laughed if the bottom half of the wood collar around his neck wasn't jamming into his esophagus.

Heavy footsteps thudded from behind him, getting closer. Looked like he had a visitor. Sure enough, Lud walked around front and bent to look Tracker in the eye.

"I hear the stocks are terrible for your back. How's it feeling?"

"Never better," Tracker replied through clenched teeth. His back was killing him. "What the hell do you want?"

"I came to fetch you for your doctor appointment."

Tracker had no idea what the jackass was talking about. "If it's about my back, really, it's fine."

Laughing, Lud straightened. "Since you're being this giant pain in the ass about knocking up Victoria—"

"Are you fucking serious?" Rage—and the wooden collar—made Tracker choke out his words. "You're on board with selling cubs, *innocent infants*, into a life of misery? Do you know what it was like for me as a youngling?"

He was practically shaking with fury made hotter by the proximity of the full moon. Never before had he welcomed it like right now. He couldn't wait to break out of his human body, to feel the agonizing crack of bone and the searing stretch of flesh that would make him the most powerful warg in the pack.

And that, he suspected, was what they all feared most. They knew his blood ran thick with *Volgy* DNA, cursed to have only one litter in a lifetime but in trade they were bigger than other wargs. Stronger. And tougher.

With his parents and siblings dead, he was King Shit. Or he would have been, if not for the fact that he was a slave. As far as rank went, he was just Shit.

And he was getting tired of it.

"Well?" he snarled at Lud. "Are you okay with sacrificing babies? With knowing that those babies, *from this pack*, will never know a moment of peace or a sliver of mercy? They'll live with empty bellies and gnawing pain. They'll feel fear with every waking breath. They'll know only violence and hatred. They'll pray for an end to the suffering. They'll pray for *death*. And you're just, what, cool with that?"

Ludwig stumbled back as the force of Tracker's words landed punches right in the other male's moral center. Shame flushed in Lud's face, sparking the tiniest bit of hope that Tracker had gotten through to him. But like a good, brainwashed minion, he got hold of himself, and a mask of indifference hardened his features within seconds.

"None of us wanted this," Lud said. "Least of all me. I was supposed to mate your sister." The mask slipped, and his gaze flitted to the ground. "But here we are. I don't want to give up any of our young, but if we don't, we will all die. If we're lucky, Victoria will only have twins." He twitched one shoulder in a half-hearted shrug. "One cub is better than four, right?"

Not to that one cub.

"You can justify it any way you want, but it's bullshit, and you know it." Tracker was going to kill this fucker. One hundred percent.

"Whatever." Lud patted Tracker's head like he was a puppy. "We gotta get you to the doc."

"What the hell for?"

Lud reached into his pocket for a set of keys. "Well, since you refuse to make babies the natural way, and since Pestilence might be coming to rescue you and slaughter us, we need to do things the hard and fast way."

"Which is," he gritted out.

"Victoria hired a demon who specializes in, shall we say, *alternative* insemination methods."

"And then?"

"Then we get rid of the goat and your female, and we send you to the slavers—"

"Where Jillian and Reseph won't be able track me, and you'll be safe."

"Yep."

Terror sliced through him like a cold knife, terror like he hadn't felt in years. He couldn't be sent back. He couldn't endure that kind of misery again.

Fear paralyzed him, left him as stunned as if he'd been poleaxed as Lud unlocked the stocks and fixed a collar and chain around his neck.

His mind shut down at the click of the restraints, hurling him into the desperate mindset of slave instinct and training. Everything inside him, his hopes, his dreams, his sense of self, withered like a dying flower as he followed Lud in a docile, dazed shuffle.

Everything Stacey had done for him seemed so distant. So unreal. He wouldn't survive this. The slave bond wouldn't allow him to take his own life, but his will to live was gone, lost in a devastating numbness.

Nothing mattered anymore. Nothing but Stacey, who might mourn him, but—

She wouldn't survive this, either.

Fear for her punched through his dazed state. He'd already failed her by letting her get taken. He couldn't fail her again. Closing his eyes, he clawed his way out of the dark pit he'd fallen into. No way would he go meekly back to the Neethul slavers.

He didn't care about his own life, but he would do what he had to in order to save hers.

A plan. He needed a plan.

He kept up the stumbling zombie walk as he took note of his surroundings. Several pack members milled about, most watching him take his perp walk toward Victoria's cabin.

What cowards.

He wondered, if he were able to overpower Lud and break free, if any of them would help him. Toss him a weapon. Like that snow shovel leaning against the fence of a nearby house.

Would any of them stand up to Victoria?

He was going to go with no.

"Lud!" Andris jogged over. "There's a truck coming. I think it's the power company."

"Shit. I forgot they were coming." He shoved Tracker's leash into Andris's hands. "Take him to Victoria. I'll handle the power guy."

Andris nodded and started walking. "Hey, man," he said, shooting Tracker a shamed look. "What your parents did was fucked up. You got a raw deal. And this whole thing is bullshit."

Tracker took a mental picture of the location of that ax near the woodshed. "Then let me go."

"I wish I could, but the pack would rip me apart." He guided them around a patch of ice. "Fucking Victoria. Between you and me, I think she's the reason your parents and brothers and sister are dead."

Tracker jerked to a halt, slipped on the ice, and nearly took a header. Only Andris's lightning-fast reflexes kept him upright when his hand shot out to catch Tracker's biceps.

"What?" He jerked out of Andris's grip. "That makes no sense. She knew the pack was at risk if they died."

Andris lowered his voice and started moving again, this time stepping to avoid getting too close to the onlookers. "I think only your parents were the targets. And maybe your sister and one of your brothers. But your brother Hunter and Victoria were going to mate."

"Still not following," he growled. He didn't have time for this. They were almost at Victoria's house.

Andris slowed down and lowered his voice to a whisper. "Some of us think she and Hunter wanted everyone out of the way so they could lead the pack. But Hunter inadvertently got caught in his own Aegis trap."

Tracker didn't bother to hide his skepticism. His family was scum, but murder-their-own scum?

Then again, his parents had sold him into slavery.

"So you think he arranged for everyone to be in the same place, at the same time, and then he tipped off The Aegis…but didn't get away?" Still sounded a little farfetched.

"Dude. Hunter arranged a big donation to the local hospital, with a ceremony and plaque and shit, all in the name of your family. Everyone was invited—a bunch of bigwig humans in Yellowknife, the pack…hospital people. But afterward, the family gathered for pictures. Alone. Away from the pack and humans at this bar he'd rented out for a private party. The rest of us returned to the village, and Victoria made this big deal about Hunter being on his way back, too, because he forgot something for the photo shoot, blah, blah."

Andris took a deep breath and offered a goofy smile to a passing female. He gave her ass a long, appraising look before continuing, and if her sudden sway was any indication, she knew it.

"Anyway," he continued, "Hunter never made it. We found out later that your family was slaughtered by the 'photographers' and 'bartenders' at the tavern, and Hunter got run off the road and killed in a ditch."

They rounded a corner and started up the street toward Victoria's house.

"So you think The Aegis betrayed him?"

"That's what they do," Andris drawled. "And now Victoria has to figure out a new way to assume power."

Well, well, wasn't that interesting. Not especially helpful, but interesting.

"I don't suppose you know what she's got planned for me with this demon doctor."

Andris snorted. "I'm not an alpha. I don't get pack briefings." He led Tracker across the street. "But I hear the plan for your female is to hunt her after we shift."

Tracker should have known. Should have guessed that if they had to kill a human, they were going to make a sport of it. Revert to the old ways of pack bonding by blood sacrifice.

None of these assholes understood what sacrifice was.

"Sick, huh?" Andris swallowed a couple of times, and Tracker wondered how many others in the pack felt the same way. "They've already loaded her up to release her somewhere. Give her a head start." He let out a bitter laugh. "Gotta make it a challenge, you know? Fucked up, man. I'm not killing a human. I'm not." He looked even sicker, now, his head hanging, his gaze landing everywhere Tracker wasn't. "Some of us are going to refuse. We'll chain ourselves overnight in protest."

"That's nice," Tracker said in a sarcastic drawl. "I'm sure it'll help. Maybe you could make some signs, too? Maybe vandalize storefronts or some mailboxes, or, I don't know, *overthrow the current leadership and do something that's actually helpful?*"

"I'm gonna be honest, dude. Our courage only goes so far. If we try that, we get killed, but only after a lot of torture. No offense, but I don't feel like suffering for you."

Tracker got that. He didn't like it, but he got it. For about two seconds, he'd once entertained the idea of a slave revolt.

For two seconds.

He didn't mind dying. But he sure as hell didn't want to come out alive on the wrong side of a coup that didn't stand a chance to begin with.

Okay, so he wouldn't get any active help from the protesters, but that would still mean fewer pack members he'd have to fight.

"How many of you are there?"

"Eight, maybe. And a few who are going to run with the pack but not participate in the kill."

So that left between about fifteen and twenty psychos to deal with.

One against twenty. Two, if he could spring Stacey.

Not good odds.

But...what if he could bring the odds into his favor?

"Andris."

"Yeah?"

"Can you get something out of my right pocket?"

The other male shot him a questioning glance, and Tracker hoped like hell he got the message he was trying to send.

Please.

Inclining his head in an almost imperceptible nod, Andris looked around, and then quickly dipped his fingers into Tracker's jeans. He fished around for a second and drew out a coin.

"In my hand."

Andris passed it to him and continued walking as if nothing had happened.

Good kid.

Tracker clenched his fist around the disc of metal Harvester had given him. She hadn't issued instructions with it, but he figured sending out mental messages while holding it was probably the thing to do.

Harvester.

He reconsidered, wondering if her angel name would be better to use than her fallen one.

Verrine. Help. Hurry.

"Come on, Andris," a deep voice called out from ahead. "Tracker should have been here five minutes ago. Victoria is going to bust something."

Tracker looked up at the enforcer waving them toward Victoria's cabin.

Hurry.

He kept up the docile act, allowing Andris to lead him into the dwelling. This time, the room wasn't full of people staring at him. Judging him. Disgusted by him.

This was worse.

Candles allowed enough light for him to make out some sort of wooden contraption in the middle of the room, complete with restraints.

Man, he hated restraints.

Breathe. Breathe. Fight. No more sliding back into slave mode. This is battle mode.

A skinny humanoid male in a gray business suit emerged from the shadows, his short, ebony horns glinting in the flicker of the candle flames. His greasy, sinister smile dropped the temperature in the room at least twenty degrees, but his horns sizzled, casting steam into the air as he moved closer.

Tracker didn't even have time to blink. The demon moved in a blur of hot fog, wrenching Tracker's bound hands up and slamming his spine against the wood rack. Locks snapped around his wrists, leaving him hanging by his arms.

Roaring in fury, he slammed both feet into the fucker, catching him in the gut. The horned business guy flew backward, crunching into the far wall and bringing down a painting and some porcelain teacups on a shelf.

He wasn't down more than half a second. Flames sprouted from the base of his horns as he hurtled across the room and nailed Tracker in the jaw so hard he saw stars and tasted blood. Pain shot through his head, circling his skull in endless spirals.

Vaguely, a metallic *tink* rung in his ears…sounded like a penny dropped on the floor.

A penny. A coin.

Shit!

Heat from the demon's horns seared Tracker as he bent to pick up Harvester's coin.

Victoria moved in from out of the shadows. "What is it?"

The demon studied it, smoothing his dark-nailed thumb over the angel wings on one side. Maybe he wouldn't know. Few would, right?

Abruptly the demon hissed and dropped the coin. "Get me a plastic bottle. Hurry!"

Victoria snapped her fingers, and an adolescent female burst from another room and darted out the door to, Tracker assumed, get a bottle.

Before the door even closed, Victoria retrieved the coin from the floor where it landed. "I said, what is it?"

The demon snatched it back from her and turned down his horns, leaving only steam and a faint sizzling noise.

"It's an angel marker."

"Is that supposed to mean something to me?" she snapped.

Tracker hung there like a piece of meat, hoping like hell that Harvester had gotten the summons. If she popped in right now, that would be really helpful.

Come on, Harvester.

The demon dragged his black gaze up and down Tracker, probably trying to figure out why a werewolf slave had a priceless possession like that.

"It allows the holder to summon the angel it belonged to," the demon said. "We have to get rid of it."

The girl burst through the front door, nearly tripping over the threshold in her haste. The demon had the bottle in his hand and the cap off before the girl came to full stop. The coin made a dull thud as it hit the plastic bottom, and Tracker felt it all the way to his gut. That coin was the only way he and Stacey were going to make it out of this alive.

He nearly puked when the demon tightened the cap and handed it back to the girl.

"Toss this into the river. Run!" The girl took off again, and as he watched her go, he said, "With any luck, the angel he summoned will materialize miles away instead of in your living room." His lips peeled away from sharklike teeth as he turned his evil gaze on Tracker. "Fool. Now we have to speed things up." He reached into a bag on the floor and pulled out a giant syringe. "This is going to sting a little…"

Chapter 16

Harvester was being summoned.

It wasn't anything new. As an angel assigned to watch over the Four Horsemen of the Apocalypse, she got summoned by them a lot. Not as often as they used to summon her back when their Seals were on the verge of breaking, but they still put in calls. Sometimes they invited her and her mate, their father, Reaver, to family get-togethers, which was nice.

Unfortunately, Reaver was in a lot of trouble for his role in the Sheoul-gra disaster last year, and the Archangel Council was restricting his movement outside of Heaven right now.

Idiots. Reaver was the most powerful angel in existence, and a battle angel to boot. He would be an extremely useful asset now that Sheoul-gra's billions of demons had been freed and were wreaking havoc.

Heaven argued that they were free *because* of Reaver.

It might be a little true, but still. You didn't sheathe your best blade during a fight.

Serious idiots.

Standing on the crystal deck of the home they shared over the Heavenly Sea of Harmony, she opened herself up to the summons. Hopefully, it was Thanatos, extending an invitation to his daughter's birthday party.

She closed her eyes and spread her arms, allowing the summons to fill her soul. As the energy expanded and tingled, the sender's individual vibration began to take form.

She frowned. It wasn't Thanatos. Or any of the Horsemen.

She waited, and gradually the vibration settled into a pattern.

Tracker.

Tracker?

Was this a mistake? He hated her. He wouldn't summon her unless—

Unless it was a serious emergency.

Shit.

Her pulse pounded as she sought the location of the coin she'd given him for, well, emergencies. Once she had a lock, she dematerialized.

She shot through the ether, a swirl of light and dark, color and nothingness. Focused on the coin, she let the tug of the summons suck her through the void of silence. The coin's signal grew stronger, became an unbearable scream at the end, and she materialized, expecting to see Tracker.

Ice cold water welcomed her instead. It rushed around her, gripping her in a powerful swell and tumbling her, head over ass, through a rush of rapids. What the—

She breached the surface, gasping for air and trying to get her bearings. How the hell was she in a river?

And where was the coin? And Tracker?

Her feet found purchase as the river widened, allowing her to slow down and follow the coin's unique vibration. Twenty yards ahead, she spotted something glinting in the sun. A soda bottle? It bobbed in the current, bouncing off rocks as it floated down the river.

She shoved off the river bottom and caught the thing before flashing herself to the rocky shore.

And there inside the bottle was the coin she'd given Tracker.

Well, this was unexpected. She had no idea why he would have put it inside a bottle and then tossed it into a river, but whatever the reason, it couldn't be good.

Fearing a trap, she weaponized herself, constructing an invisible bubble of energy that would electrocute anyone dumb enough to attack her. She didn't sense evil nearby…but evil was sneaky. She knew firsthand, seeing how she used to be evil.

Also, her dad was Satan, so there was that.

When nothing jumped out at her, she poofed herself dry and focused on where she was. Her built-in GPS told her she was in Canada. Somewhere near Yellowknife.

Why would Tracker be here? Wait…tonight was the full moon. Was his pack nearby? The last she knew, they'd been in Hungary. No, wait…Wyoming?

Her gut twisted. She didn't know. She hadn't paid that much attention to him when he'd been her charge.

Guilt raked her with its sharp claws. Yes, there'd been a reason she'd been such a monster back then, but it didn't change the fact that he'd paid a big price for the choices she'd been forced to make.

She totally deserved his hatred.

Okay, so what now? She couldn't sense him, but she should be able to sense a pack of werewolves if she got close enough.

Taking a deep breath, she launched into the air with a powerful sweep of her wings. Birds scattered as she punched through a low deck of clouds and headed north, toward Yellowknife. The pack would, most likely, be within driving distance of the town. They'd want to be remote for privacy and moon runs, but they'd also want to be close enough to shop and work.

A sense of urgency drove her, compelled her to fly as fast as her wings would allow. She'd done the best she could for Tracker when she'd transferred his slave bond to Jillian, but that hadn't made up for years of torment.

She could make up for it now.

Hold on, Tracker. I'm coming.

Chapter 17

The ride in the back of the pickup made Stacey wish she was still trapped in the murder shed.

She'd been blindfolded, gagged, and her wrists and ankles bound. All before being thrown into the bed of a freezing truck and driven over roads that must have been bombed. She'd been tossed around like a sad little tuber in a game of Pass the Potato.

Already bruised and sore, she cursed when the vehicle came to a sudden stop, throwing her up against the cab of the truck.

Then things got worse.

At least when the truck was moving, nothing horrible was happening. But now that it had stopped, something horrible *was* going to happen.

Because if those people she overheard were right, she was about to be hunted.

Two doors opened and closed. Heavy footsteps. Two sets. The tailgate clanged, and then hands clamped around her ankles and yanked her out of the truck.

She hit the ground like a sack of flour, the gag muffling her cry of pain as her shoulder wrenched. Then it muffled her shouted, "Asshole!"

Chuckling, her captor dragged her across the frozen ground and sticks that poked her in the butt and back. What sadistic fucks. Were they trying to tenderize her before they ate her?

It seemed like they'd dragged her for a hundred yards when they finally stopped, propped her up against a tree, and removed the blindfold.

She blinked in the early evening sunlight and waited for her vision to clear. The gag followed, and a dude with red hair and a scraggly beard bent to look her in the eyes.

"You okay?"

Seemed like an odd thing to ask someone after you'd just brutalized them, but she'd play along.

"Never better. Except all my entire life when I wasn't bound, gagged, blindfolded, and tossed around like a piece of meat in preparation for being hunted. But, you know, otherwise, I'm just fine."

Okay, maybe she hadn't exactly played along. But dammit, this situation sucked.

She heard laughter from near the truck, and she looked over to see a dark-haired guy in a red flannel shirt flipping up the tailgate of a beat-up white Ford.

"I like her," he said. "It's a shame we have to get rid of her."

Redbeard shrugged. "Our pack hasn't celebrated the old ways in decades. I think this'll be good for us. Remind everyone of our roots. We've become too civilized. Victoria is going to change things."

"I don't know, man." Redshirt swung around. "You ever heard that saying 'adapt or die'? The Aegis and DART aren't fucking around when it comes to putting down rogue wargs. Or entire warg packs. Did you hear about that pack in Russia that got wiped out in one night? Three dozen dead."

"Yeah, well, if it gets out that we have one of the Four Horsemen's friends, what do you think is gonna happen to us?" Redbeard gestured to Stacey. "We gotta get rid of the evidence. Might as well do it the way our ancestors did it."

"You're sick," she spat.

A crooked smile twisted his lips as he bent and once more got to eye level. "And you're going to be dinner." He straightened and looked at his buddy. "Let's go. We'll meet the pack back at the square, and as soon as we shift, we hunt."

"So you're just going to leave me here?"

Redbeard stared at her like she was a child who was unable to grasp an adult concept. "See, sweetie, this is how a hunt works. You run, and we find you." He pointed to her ankles. "That's why I freed you. There's no point of a hunt if you're tied up in one place."

Redshirt nodded. "True. It would be unsportsmanlike to leave you tied up. I mean, we don't even bait deer. We hunt them with honor."

"Oh, well, that makes it all better," she snapped. "If honor is so important to you, how about you take the ropes off my wrists too."

Redbeard looked hesitant, but Redshirt spoke up. "We should. She should at least be able to defend herself if she gets attacked by a mountain lion or something."

"Definitely," Stacey said. "You wouldn't want me to get eaten by a big cat before you guys get me, right?"

Redbeard cursed, but he reached into his pocket and pulled out a knife. Roughly, he jerked her away from the tree and sawed at the ropes. Finally, her hands sprung free, and her shoulders screamed in both relief and agony as the blood flow and feeling returned to them.

She sucked in a few calming breaths as they hopped into the truck and started it up. Redshirt looked back at her as they drove away, but Redbeard didn't so much as glance in the rearview mirror.

She stayed put until she no longer heard the rumble of the engine.

Now what?

She was in the middle of nowhere, with nothing but trees and snow all around. Snowcapped mountaintops rose up over the canopy of trees in the distance, but since she didn't know where she was, she had no idea what mountains they were or if there would be people nearby. It was a safe bet that the psychos hadn't dumped her near a settlement, and she had a feeling that no matter how far and how fast she went, she wouldn't find help.

Shivering, she lifted the hood on the parka they'd given her and started off in a random direction. Hopefully she could find a river where the snow had been scoured away on the banks enough that she could walk without leaving a trail. Not that werewolves couldn't track by scent. But if worse came to worst, she could always throw herself in the river to get away. Assuming the river was thawed.

Yes, she would freeze to death or drown.

But either of those things would be way, way better than being torn apart for a meal.

* * * *

Tracker snarled in pain and outrage as the demon jabbed a big-ass needle into his gut.

Victoria, who had been standing nearby, arms folded over her chest, let out a curse. "Is that really necessary? We don't want his master to be drawn by his pain."

"Humans don't feel a slave's misery through the bond like demons do. And yes, it's necessary. This will increase sperm production." The demon withdrew the syringe. "I'll take the semen using another needle."

Tracker's balls climbed up into his abdomen. "That sounds painful."

The demon smiled. "It is."

Victoria sighed. "Can't we do this the old-fashioned way? You already injected me with fertility drugs to trigger the breeding heat."

"No," Tracker growled, "we can't." He'd rather play pincushion.

"Actually," the demon said, "we can." He dug through his bag of medical crap and held up a vile of neon green liquid. "This is a serum made from the seminal fluid of a post-*s'genesis* Seminus demon."

"What's a Seminus demon?" Victoria asked.

Tracker knew, but only because Jillian and Reseph were friends with some. "The word 'semen' is right in their name. What do you think?"

The demon ignored Tracker and addressed Victoria. "They're a breed of incubus that must have sex or die. This serum makes males desperate. Tracker won't be able to control himself around any female."

Victoria's gaze grew dark with hunger as she eyed Tracker. "What's post-*s'genesis*?"

Tracker was curious about that too. Not enough to ask these fucks, but curiosity kept his mind busy, and right now, that was a welcome break.

The demon held up the vial to the light of a candle and studied it as he spoke. "It's a life stage, a transformation that makes them fertile. It also makes them mad with uncontrollable lust. Injecting the serum I made into every species I've tested it on made them temporarily fertile and mindless with the need to screw."

"It won't kill him, will it?"

"It hasn't killed any of my test subjects," he said with a shrug. "I'd say it's perfectly safe."

"Says the demon," Tracker muttered.

"Yes," the demon mused. "Says the demon." He paused. "I *am* a doctor, you know."

"You work at Underworld General?"

The demon cackled as he removed a fresh syringe from a package. "With those arrogant elitists? I don't think so."

Tracker's bark of laughter jolted his body, making his shoulders creak in agony, but he didn't care. Just made him angrier, and he was banking that shit. "So they wouldn't hire you, huh?"

The demon's expression said Tracker's jab had struck a nerve. "I run my own, very lucrative business, cur."

No doubt he did. Tracker had seen dozens of shoddily run "clinics" in Sheoul, where all manner of demons practiced various forms of medicine.

The demon punched the syringe's needle into the vial's rubber stopper and withdrew the green liquid. When he pulled it free, the muted pop sent a chill up Tracker's spine.

"How long until it takes effect?" Victoria asked. "We will be shifting in about thirty minutes."

The doctor looked at his watch and moved to Tracker. "Almost instantly. You should be able to get the deed done before you shift. If not, I'll chain him and take what I need. We can impregnate you after you shift back."

"That's cutting it pretty close." Victoria worried her bottom lip as she eyed her watch. "We need to get him back to the slavers as soon as possible so his master can't track us, let alone the angel he summoned."

The demon jabbed Tracker in the arm with the needle, and a burning sensation spread from the site through his veins. Almost instantly, his groin lit on fire, an agony that was both painful and pleasant.

Thoughts of Stacey filled his head. The memory of what they'd done in the barn became his entire world as the rest of it fell away. He could still hear the activity around him, could still feel his wrists and feet so tightly bound that they'd lost sensation. But his mind was in an erotic fantasy that was growing more intense by the second.

Distantly, he heard a female voice. "Looks like it's working."

"That was fast," came a male voice. "Let's get him down. We can tie him to the bed to be safe."

Yes, tied to the bed. If Stacey wanted to tie him to the mouth of an active volcano, he'd be cool with it. She could restrain him in any way she wanted…

Tugs on his arms and legs told him the restraints were being loosened, and then arms caught him as he fell forward.

"Hurry," the doctor said. "He'll start regaining his senses any minute now. You do not want a pissed-off sex maniac attacking you."

"Speak for yourself, demon," Victoria said in a low, sensual voice that dripped with erotic promise and made Tracker's cock twitch.

Thoughts of Stacey faded as his focus narrowed on the female in the room, the one who was fertile and aroused. She watched him, their gazes locking like two streams of liquid fire.

"Are you sure we need to restrain him," she breathed.

"It would be wise."

Absently, she trailed a finger along her cleavage, and through the haze of need, Tracker wondered if the injection also made him give off an aphrodisiac via his skin or breath. Because she was definitely turned on.

"I think I can handle him." She popped the top button, leaving more creamy flesh exposed. "Leave us."

"But—"

"Leave us!" She gestured to the door. "Send everyone but the enforcers to the staging meadow for the moon shift. If I'm not there by the time they shift, tell them to hunt. I'll catch up."

The two males who had been holding him up released him, and without their support, his legs gave out and he hit the floor on his knees. His pelvis ached, his cock hurt, and his entire body was strung out with the need for sex.

Was this how Seminus demons lived their lives? Because it sucked. All he could think about was getting between a female's legs. All he wanted was to sink deep in her heat and pump until he came over and over.

Stacey.

He wanted Stacey.

But she wasn't here. His brain fuzzed out as lust warred with the confusion and questions in his head. Where was she?

We're going to hunt her.

Hunt her? Now he remembered. These assholes were going to kill her.

Agony pierced his groin as a stab of need went through him like a lightning bolt. Instinctively he realized that if he didn't find release, the pain would get worse.

Good thing he'd learned to live with pain because he was going to use it. He was going to fuck some people up, and then he was going to find Stacey.

And he was going to claim her.

Screw the slavers. She. Was. His.

Chapter 18

Tracker was alone with her.

Victoria.

She stood near the door to the bedroom, her blouse unbuttoned to reveal full breasts held up by a black satin bra that made Tracker's mouth water.

Because all he could think about was Stacey in the same bra.

She'd be beautiful. He'd wrap his hands around her waist and rip through the bra with his teeth. Or claws.

He looked down at his hands and clenched them as the full moon made his blood heat. It wouldn't be long now. Then the ultimate ecstasy would be upon him, the agony of the shift, the pure joy at becoming a creature that lived life as if on steroids. Everything was heightened times a thousand, every one of his senses.

Except pain. That was the one thing that dulled. It allowed him to fight harder. Fight longer. Live better.

But right now he was still vulnerable, and the sting of desire was wrenching his insides and turning his mind to mush.

"Come on, Tracker," Victoria crooned as she ran her palm down her flat, hard abs to the waistband of her jeans. She let her fingers play with the button, teasing him, before she flicked it open and peeled the fly away to reveal a hint of black lace beneath.

Stacey's underwear had lace.

He groaned at the thought, and his cock pressed even harder against the prison of his jeans.

"Yes," she purred. "I can sense your desire."

Oh, there was desire, all right. Desire to take Stacey like an animal.

And desire to kill Victoria.

Piercing cramps stabbed him in the groin at that thought. He needed sex, not death, and his body knew it. His mind might be obsessed with Stacey, but his Seminus-hijacked body demanded he take any female it could find.

A growl issued from deep in his throat as he moved toward her. Kill. Fuck. Kill. Fuck.

Son of a—

He stumbled to a halt, refusing to take another step until he could get his body and mind to coordinate. But if the pain and desperation was any clue, it wouldn't happen. He had to get out of here. Away from Victoria.

Snarling, he wheeled around and bolted for the front door. On the cusp of moon fever, he embraced the intensifying strength it gave him and ripped the door from its hinges.

Cold air rushed in, cooling his heated skin and allowing him to focus, for just a second, on the activity outside.

There were half a dozen enforcers, plus the demon, who'd remained behind when the others left to shift for the hunt. They were milling around, waiting.

Waiting for Victoria to come outside and say the deed was done so Tracker could be delivered to the slavers.

Never. He couldn't go back there. He couldn't be transferred to anyone else again.

I'll die first.

With a roar, he launched himself into the crowd.

He caught them by surprise and laid out two big males before anyone was able to even get close to him.

A sucker punch came in from behind, but he whirled and dropped the fucker with a leaping roundhouse kick to the neck.

Thank you, Reseph.

Countless hours of combat training had paid off. The Horseman had taught him well.

Through the fog of sexual need and hate-filled rage, he attacked everyone in sight, throwing off those who tried to take him to the ground. Fists met flesh, kicks cracked bone.

The demon doctor barreled toward him, his horns ten times bigger than before and coated in flame. Tracker flung himself to the pavement and rolled out of his path, but the move cost him. Outnumbered, he found himself pinned by three males.

"Hold him!"

"Dammit, knock him out!"

"I said—"

Suddenly, the guys flew off him and landed in heaps a few yards away. Tracker flipped to his feet, teeth bared and bloody, fists clenched.

All around him, bodies were strewn like rag dolls.

The demon lay on the sidewalk. His head lay a few feet away. Next to him, her neck twisted at an unnatural angle, was Victoria.

And standing in the middle of the street, hands on her slim hips, was an angel. And, as usual, she looked like anything *but* an angel in a midnight leather corset, black form-fitting tights, and knee-high boots with hot pink laces.

"Nice work," Harvester said as she surveyed the area. "All that icy swimming for nothing. You didn't need to summon me after all."

Tracker panted through a wave of erotic agony. "Clearly, I did."

"No, actually, you didn't. Sometimes I can see glimpses of the future seconds before it happens." She shrugged. "It's an angel upgrade. Anyway, you would have taken them all out. You went cray-cray. Must be the *Volgy* bloodline. You're probably a zillion times stronger on *Volgy*-claimed land." She pointed to the snow shovel against the staircase. "You'd have done the beheading with that." She waved in the direction of Victoria's body. "That ho-bag? Bare hands. You're pretty badass, Tracker. I'd give you a blow-by-blow of all of them if I hadn't just done all of this myself in order to move things along." Dark brow furrowed, she lay her hand on him, and he swayed toward her, his body craving the feel of female skin on his. "What have they done to you?"

"They took…" He gulped a breath. "They took my female."

She blinked in surprise. "You have a female? Huh. What about you? What did they do?"

"Injection." He panted through another cramp of need, but this time it was joined by the familiar muscle spasms that heralded the imminent moon shift. "Seminus demon juice or something."

"Oh." She made a face. "Yikes. Guess you'd better find your female."

He groaned as his muscles tightened in preparation of transformation. "Harvester, I need you to promise me something."

"Promises aren't my thing, but what is it you want?"

"If I'm ever taken away from Jillian, kill me." He doubled over, clutching his gut and cursing the demon doctor. "I can't…I can't go back to the slaver guild. I can't belong to another master. Please, I don't care how long it takes to find me, do it. End me."

"That's silly." She waved her hand in dismissal. "I'll simply kill whoever has you, and the bond will transfer to me. I'll find you another decent master."

"I don't want to live like this," he shouted. "Never again. Promise me, Harvester."

Harvester swallowed, her long, slender neck undulating over and over. Finally, reluctantly, she nodded.

"Thank you," he rasped, his voice ravaged by the lengthening of his own throat as the werewolf shift took hold. He gestured toward Rick, who stood tethered in a yard down the street. "Will you take him back to Jillian's?"

She eyed the goat. "Seriously? Do I look like a farmhand—" She snapped her mouth shut and pasted on a resigned, pained smile. "Sure. Anything for you. Do you need anything else?"

Now when he spoke, it was through jaws half-formed with werewolf teeth and a snout. "They have my female. But that…that I have handled."

Joints popped, bones broke, and his skin stretched as the transformation finished. Within moments, he was bigger. Stronger. Standing on two thick, furred legs, and way more pissed off.

Harvester stood by, watching as he put his nose to the air and sought the scent of his pack. They'd be heading in the direction of Stacey.

There. They'd gone north. With a howl, he went down on all fours and took off. He just hoped he was in time.

* * * *

Sonorous howls rang out in the night, hanging creepily long in the still air. Terror skated over the surface of Stacey's skin as she stumbled to a stop on the game trail she'd been following.

They were getting closer.

Panting, gasping for breath, she braced herself on a tree trunk as she scanned for movement in the shadows. Nightfall had enveloped the forest, but the moon and cloudless sky made it seem like daytime. Daytime in a black and white movie.

Like the horror movie she was currently living in.

The couple that has sex always dies.

Another resonant howl drifted in from her right, and she jumped.

It's probably just wolves. Normal wolves. Normal wolves don't eat people. It's all fine.

That was what she'd been repeating to herself as she ran. Despite their undeserving reputation, wolves didn't usually mess with humans, so as long as she kept telling herself the howls that were coming closer were human-realm wild canines, all was good.

But man, she'd never heard wolves that sounded like this. That made her blood turn to gel and her marrow freeze solid.

Maybe Canadian wolves had a different howl than Colorado wolves. Maybe their vocalizations were deeper, louder, and more bloodcurdling.

Yeah, she'd go with that.

More howls joined the others, coming from behind and to the side of her. Then more. Closer.

They were herding her.

Lungs burning, she took off again in a desperate sprint, running toward the distant sound of rushing water. Branches slapped at her face as she ran, and twice she fell over logs, but nothing slowed her. Not even pain. Hell, she had so much adrenaline in her body she'd probably never feel pain again.

More howls.

Even closer.

Oh, God.

Ahead, a doe leaped onto the trail, glanced at Stacey with eyes wild with terror, and then crashed away through the forest.

Don't worry, pretty girl. This time, you're not the prey.

Exhausted, she pushed hard, but she was slowing down. Thickets and low branches grabbed at her, tearing her clothes and skin.

She was leaving her scent like breadcrumbs.

A series of way-too-close howls nearly made her scream.

She had no remaining bursts of speed. Gritting her teeth, she pushed through cramps in her side and calf.

Then, ahead, beyond the edge of a clearing, she saw hard angles. Unnatural angles.

Man made.

Please, please let it be people.

She lurched toward the structure, could make out twin ruts coming out of the forest, dents in the patchy snow. Tire tracks?

As she got closer, the outline of a small building took shape. An outhouse? No, not with windows. High, small windows meant to keep bears from getting through them.

A cabin!

She sobbed in relief as hope gave her one last burst of energy. She sprinted across the clearing, slipping and sliding on patches of snow and partially frozen mud.

Hurry, hurry…

She reached the little log cabin, a hunting shack, most likely, and practically slammed into the door. Her breath came in searing whips of air and her brain was starved of the oxygen she needed to think, but she knew she'd have to break a window to get in.

Still, she tried the door.

Holy shit, it was unlocked.

Whoever owned the place probably didn't think many people would be out here to vandalize it. Or they figured that if someone needed an emergency shelter, they were welcome to it.

Thank you, whoever you are.

The heavy door creaked open, and she practically fell inside. Closing the thing took more effort than she'd have liked, and once closed, she collapsed against it, her body finally giving out.

She gave herself until the count of ten to catch her breath, and then she fumbled with the deadbolt and secured the door.

It was dark inside, but the two windows allowed enough moonlight for her to make out a beat-up couch on the far wall. And to realize there was no back door.

This was, basically, a big coffin.

The windows were too small for the beasts to crawl through, but they'd eventually break down the door.

The couch might buy her a little time if she could drag it over to block the entrance. Still panting, she limped over to drag it, a few inches at a time. Took forever, but she finally got it against the door.

Okay. Weapons. She needed weapons.

Desperately, she searched the small space for something better than the rusty saw tooth she'd tucked in her pocket before the goons threw her in the pickup.

She started with the kitchen, which turned up a haul of blades, including a fourteen-inch hunting knife. A tin box near the wood stove held a hatchet and an ax.

For the first time since this nightmare began, she felt like she might have a chance of surviving. Depending on how many werewolves there were and how long the door held out.

Holding onto hope but also holding her breath, she peeked out the window.

Nothing so far. Thank G—

Movement. Along the edge of the forest.

The shadows writhed and undulated, until the things making the shadows slipped out of the woods.

And they were definitely not wolves.

One by one, monstrous creatures, some on all fours and some upright on two legs, crept into the clearing. The leader stopped a hundred yards away. Going up on his two hind legs, he lifted his massive head to the sky and howled, an ear shattering blast of terror that made Stacey cry out.

As his howl died down, he turned his attention toward the cabin. The leader's stare burned right into her eyes as he began a slow, almost taunting lope.

Stacey spun away from the window and grabbed the ax.

Then they were there. Sniffing at the base of the door. Scratching.

Her heart beat so fast she thought she might pass out.

The doorknob jiggled.

Oh, God.

An enormous white head appeared in the window. Hot breath fogged the bottom half of the glass, and glowing eyes dominated the top.

It was looking right at her.

And she swore it was laughing.

Every drop of her law enforcement and DART training forgotten, she seized up. She'd fought a few demons in her life, had confronted a lot of dangerous criminals. But in all those instances, she'd been the hunter.

She just learned how different it was to be the hunted.

The window smashed inward, and a massive, furry arm with six-inch claws reached for her, missing her throat by a whisper. Finally, oh, fucking finally, muscle memory and instinct kicked in, and with a roar of fear and fury, she went on the offensive.

She swung the ax as the beast thrust his head through the window. The heavy blade crunched into the creature's skull, right between its stunned eyes. The shockwave tore up her arm and jolted her shoulders as the thing yelped in shock and pain, blood splashing all over its snowy fur.

With a spastic jerk, it fell backward, taking the ax with it.

Everything went quiet for a moment. A long, tense, still moment. Stacey wasn't even sure her heart beat.

Then, a symphony of mournful and enraged howls shook the night. Something bashed against the door. Again. And again.

The crack of wood split the air, and the next hit tore out the door's top hinge.

Stacey tucked the butcher knife into her waistband and readied the hatchet.

She figured she had, at the most, sixty seconds before the door failed.

And she had ten seconds after that to live.

Chapter 19

Tracker tore through the wilderness with a ferocious, single-minded purpose.

Save his mate and kill her pursuers.

Okay, yeah, that was two things. But one led to the other.

He ran at top speed, the fear of being too late whipping at him like any one of his former masters.

If he was too late…

He roared in agony. He needed his mate. Not only for the sexual desires that were burning hot in his blood, but for life itself.

Belonging to Jillian had taught him that it was possible to live without fear and pain. Belonging to Stacey had taught him it was possible to *live.*

In his beast form, he retained all the normal thoughts and memories, unlike turned werewolves, who became mindless monsters. But instinct and beast mode still took hold of him, and all he could think about was tearing flesh and fur from her attackers. He wanted their blood on his tongue and their screams in his ears.

He breathed in the scent of his pack mates as he ran, keeping on the trail. Every once in a while he caught a whiff of Stacey, and he'd dig deep for even more speed.

She'd led them on quite the chase, taking them along steep, rocky cliffs and into brush-choked ravines. She'd gotten further than he'd have believed, but he knew he was at the end of it when snarls and growls filtered through the trees from the path ahead.

Then came a single, bloodcurdling scream.

Stacey.

He shot out of the forest and into a clearing torn up by clawed feet and one Stacey-sized pair of boots.

Just beyond the far edge, no fewer than a dozen werewolves clawed and chewed at a log cabin. A big silver male, Brynn, was throwing himself against the twisted door as two others ripped at the base of it, tossing aside chunks of wood as they dug.

The two windows had been broken out, and under one of them, Lud, in his human form, lay crumpled, an ax protruding from his split skull.

Fuck, yeah.

Way to go, Stacey.

He was ninety yards away. Brynn punched through the top half of the door.

Eighty yards away. A hatchet sailed through the doorway and impaled in Brynn's shoulder.

Yes!

Seventy yards away. Brynn fell back, but Nils, a scrawny, blond-furred elder, took his place and forced his way over whatever barrier kept the entire door from fully caving in.

Fifty yards away. Stacey screamed.

Forty.

Thirty. Nils leaped through the open door.

Twenty. Sienna, a red female, followed.

Ten. Brynn tossed the hatchet aside and started through the door.

Tracker vaulted through the doorway, ripping away Brynn's flank with a single, powerful strike. Brynn yelped and hit the floor with a crash.

Something slammed him in the back, and he banked hard, came around to take out John's throat with his claws before the old bastard could gather a cry of pain in it.

Tracker spun back to where Nils had Stacey pinned to the wall with his claws around her throat. Saliva dripped from his teeth as he bared them an inch from her face.

Sienna went up on her hind legs and prepared to strike a death blow with her claw-tipped paw.

In a powerful leap, Tracker hit them both from the side, taking them down like bowling pins. The impact flung Stacey aside, and Tracker heard the sickening strike of human flesh hitting the wall.

He couldn't go to her, couldn't even spare a glance. Sienna nailed him, hitting him in the chest as Nils's jaws clamped down on his back leg. Someone else hit him from behind.

He knew he should be feeling pain as they ripped into him, but he had nothing to spare but anger. Anger and love that he used to fuel the battle.

Roaring in rage, he drilled his claws into Sienna's exposed belly. She doubled over and he punched upward, catching her by the throat. Twisting, he crashed them into the couch, breaking Nils's hold on his leg.

Momentarily stunned, Sienna was slow to recover, and Tracker chomped down on her throat. She gasped, struggled, all four sets of her claws raking at him as she fought for her life.

Then Nils was there again, his teeth crunching down on the back of Tracker's neck. Pain spiraled down the entire length of his spine and up to his skull. His jaws opened, and he lost his grip on Sienna.

She jackknifed up and bit down on his throat.

Pain and darkness closed in.

"*No!*" Stacey's scream sounded distant, fuzzy.

Then Nils's weight fell away, and Tracker was only battling Sienna. He raked her, tore at her, but it wasn't until he took out an eye that she finally let go.

He sucked air as he spun around and crouched, ready to take out Nils.

But it was too late. Stacey had buried a knife to its hilt in the back of his neck, and as he stumbled around, grabbing at it blindly, she sank another into his chest.

Nils keeled over, but Stacey wasn't done.

"Bastard!" she shouted, as she wrenched the knife free and plunged it into him again.

Sienna, one paw over her destroyed eye, went for Stacey, but Tracker beat her there. With one powerful swipe, he tore out the warg's throat.

She collapsed to the blood-wet floor as he threw himself in front of Stacey, knowing that the rest of the pack was going to file in now. If he and Stacey could take them out one by one at the choke point—

His muscles turned to jelly, and he collapsed next to Sienna. What the hell…his leg, oh, shit. The back of one leg had been ripped out. He'd been hamstrung.

"Tracker!" Stacey started for him, but she hadn't gotten two steps before a blonde female dove through the door, her gaping jaws aimed for Stacey's throat.

Blondie never made it.

Suddenly, she just dropped dead. Fell out of the air mid-leap, landing at Stacey's feet.

And when he looked up, standing in the doorway like a guardian angel, was Harvester.

* * * *

Stacey was too numb and exhausted to be alarmed by the scantily clad chick in the doorway.

After all, could the newcomer really be worse than the werewolves that had tried to eat her?

Stacey stumbled back a step and sank down next to Tracker, who panted as he crouched near Nils's body, one big shoulder braced against the wall.

"Looks like I was just in time," the woman said.

"In time for what?"

"To save your lives, obvs."

Tracker's big muzzle nudged at Stacey's hand as if telling her it was okay. She stroked her hand down his face, marveling at how soft his sandy fur was. And how *big* he was.

But there was so much blood, and Stacey didn't know how to help. Hopefully the newcomer did.

"Who are you?" she asked.

"My name's Harvester." She sauntered inside, her fuck-me boots striking the wood flooring like a dominatrix's riding crop.

This was an *angel*?

"How did you find us?"

One dark eyebrow climbed up her forehead. "The first time or this time?"

"Ah…"

Harvester went down on her heels to rest her hand on Stacey's shoulder. Instantly, a warm, tingly feeling spread from the angel's palm and down her body. A stinging sensation sifted through her injuries, and to her amazement, the cuts closed and the aches began to fade.

"Tracker summoned me the first time. This time I followed him." She looked up at Tracker as he came unsteadily to two feet, clearly favoring one mangled leg. "Don't worry. I took the goat back. And I didn't kill the wargs back at the village that were chained up. I can go back though—"

Tracker growled, which Stacey assumed meant no.

"Touchy," Harvester murmured. She smiled at Stacey and pulled her to her feet. "You're as healed as I can get you."

"What about Tracker?" Damn, he was huge. Standing upright, he was at least eight feet tall. Gently, Stacey smoothed her hand down his side and flank, careful to avoid the dozens of deep gashes and the gaping wound in the back of one muscular leg. His breathing grew heavier, raspier, and she pulled her hand away, worried she was hurting him.

"Most of his wounds will heal when he shifts back. The bigger problem is that he's been injected with some sort of sex demon juice, and *that* won't be fixed by a shift back into human form."

"Sex demon juice? Um…what?"

Rubbing her chin thoughtfully, Harvester didn't appear to have heard her. "Hmm. I guess I can get you to tomorrow."

"Tomorrow?" Were all angels this hard to follow? Stacey was so confused.

"Somewhere in the world where it's morning." She gestured to Tracker. "Or do you want him ravaging you like that?"

Stacey eyed the beast next to her. Tracker, his chest heaving, his clawed fists clenching, was the epitome of power. And between his furred legs…he was erect. *Hugely* erect.

Oh, my. And…no.

Totally wrong species.

"Where will you take us?"

Harvester considered that. "Hold on. Two seconds."

She flashed away, taking the energy in the room with her. Suddenly, post-battle fatigue set in as Stacey's adrenaline levels crashed and the shock wore off, and her legs gave out. Tracker caught her in his strong arms and hauled her against his chest. Through his thick fur, she felt his heart pounding.

Felt a new, erotic energy spin up.

Tingles spread across her skin, and little fires sparked in all her erogenous zones. How could Tracker's touch, especially after such a horrific event, be affecting her like this?

The sex demon juice? Battle lust?

Harvester appeared before Stacey could come to any conclusions.

"Come on, lovebirds." She gripped Tracker's shoulder, and suddenly they were in a luxurious hotel room with sunlight streaming through giant windows that overlooked a huge city.

"Madrid," Harvester said. "It'll be morning in Colorado in about eight hours. I'll pick you up then and take you home." She wiggled her fingers at them. "Have fun, kids."

The angel flashed out of there as Tracker lowered her to her feet. When she turned to face him, the transformation had already begun.

He grunted as his body jerked and morphed, the fur melting away, replaced by firm, tan skin. His jaw shortened, his fangs receded, and within about thirty seconds, he stood before her.

Naked. His body glistening with perspiration. His cock distended and engorged.

As sexy as he was, the blood caked on his skin reminded her that they'd just come from a life-or-death situation, and as if her thoughts were printed on her forehead, his gaze softened, grew worried.

"You're…hurt," he growled.

"No, I—" She looked down at herself, at her torn and bloody clothes. Some of the blood belonged to the werewolves, but at that moment, every injury she'd taken began to ache despite Harvester's healing.

Tracker reached for her. "You need a shower and rest."

"But you need…" She swallowed.

"*You* are the priority, Stacey." He spoke through gritted teeth as a wave of what she could only describe as erotic energy flowed through him and washed over her. "The shift seems to have…reduced the need. A little."

"You know," she said, as she rested her palm on his chest, "we can do two things at once in the shower."

"We'll see." His voice was gruff but his grip gentle as he led her to the luxury bathroom with a shower the size of the entire bathroom in her rented place.

Once there, he undressed her with gentle hands. Hands she'd seen tear ferocious beasts to shreds. But with her, they were tender, peeling off her ruined shirt and torn jeans with care.

He helped her into the black and gold marble shower, and under the hot spray he washed her, massaging shampoo into her hair with such expertise she moaned.

"Where did you learn that?" Instantly, she regretted asking, but it was too late.

"Some of my masters made me wash their hair."

Her heart quivered in her chest. "Oh, Tracker."

"Shh. I should thank them. For once, something good is coming from my past."

That was the last straw. The last two days of exhaustion and terror came back to her in a wave of stress and pain. Added to the adrenaline crash, she lost it. Tears streamed down her face as she turned into Tracker and clung to him, sobbing uncontrollably.

"I'm sorry," he murmured into her hair. "I'm so sorry. I did this, and—"

"No," she said, pulling back to look him in the eye. "Don't be sorry. None of what happened is your fault. The blame lies with a bunch of scumbags in your pack, evil asshole masters, and parents who shouldn't have been allowed to breed." She placed her soapy palm on his chest to connect them through their pulses. "You are honorable and decent, and I've never met anyone like you."

"I'm not honorable and decent," he growled. "Or I wouldn't want you the way I do."

"That," she said, as she slid her hand down his chest, his rock-hard abs, and between his hip bones, "is a matter of opinion." She gripped his hard shaft, loving the way he hissed, his entire body jerking.

"We shouldn't," he breathed. "You're hurt, and I don't know if I can be gentle."

"I don't want gentle," she insisted. "I want you. Right here. Right now."

"But—"

She shut him up by dropping to her knees and swiping her tongue over the tip of his cock. The sound that came from him, something between a hiss and a moan, made her smile as she did it again, this time taking it slow. Her tongue caressed the silky smooth cap in long, lazy swirls, each one making her clench her thighs to soothe her own growing arousal.

"Stace—"

She shut him up again by taking him fully into her mouth, and this time he barked out a garbled curse and threw one hand out to brace himself on the wall. She loved his response, loved how he felt in her hand and against her lips as she sucked him.

Desire sizzled between her legs, but this was about him right now, and she brought her other hand up to fondle his sac, pinching lightly as she pumped his shaft and curled her tongue over the mushroom head.

Looking up at him, she basked in the sight of a man at the height of pleasure, his panting breaths coming from between his slightly parted lips, his face flushed, his fierce eyes locked on her, mesmerized and glittering with passion.

With a tortured groan, he threw his head back and started rocking his hips. "Now," he rasped, and he orgasmed, his entire body jerking, trembling.

She took it all, his sensitive flesh twitching when she teased him out with light flicks of her tongue.

"Holy shit." He swallowed over and over, his head still rocked back, his chest heaving with heavy breaths.

And he was still hard.

Finally, he looked down at her and pulled her to her feet. "That was…wow." He gently pushed her back against the same wall and smoothed his hand between her legs, and she damned near came from just that. When he inserted two fingers inside her wet heat, she quivered, on the very verge.

"I want you inside me," she whispered.

He shook his head. "If the demon was right, I could be fertile. We can only do it this way." He leaned in and nibbled her lobe. "Or with my mouth."

Yesssss.

Wait. Fertile. Okay, that was an interesting bit of news that dampened her desire a bit.

"So you're saying that we'll have to use condoms from now on?" She could go back on the pill too.

His fingers began a leisurely slide in and out, and hey, there was the desire again. She rocked into his hand with a moan.

"It's only temporary."

Temporary? Reaching down, she stilled his hand. "So after today you will never be able to have children, right?"

"After today, my fertility will be in the hands of the Neethul Slaver Guild."

Bastards.

Stacey wanted kids. And she wanted Tracker. What if this was their one chance to have it all? No, the timing wasn't perfect, but their relationship would never be perfect either, not when he would forever be shackled to a master.

"Okay, this is going to sound crazy, but…would it be a terrible thing if I got pregnant?"

Tracker backed up so fast she nearly fell over. "What?"

Steam rose all around them, billowing around his face and giving him an ethereal quality that drew her closer to him, to this magnificent creature who had fascinated her from the moment she'd laid eyes on him.

"This might be your only chance. *Our* only chance."

"I don't know how to be a father. I don't know anything about kids."

"No one does until they have one." She scooted up to him so her breasts were pressed against his chest and her belly was cradling his hard sex. "I love you, Tracker. I want your baby inside me. Trust me when I say that I've never wanted anything more." Reaching down, she took him in her palm. "Make me yours," she whispered.

A smoky, erotic growl rattled his chest, and then he had her up against the wall, his hands on her butt to lift her. With a shout of pure joy, she wrapped her arms around his shoulders and her legs around his waist as he penetrated her.

Their lovemaking was fast, frenzied, and she came three times before it was over and they collapsed, tangled together on the teak bench beneath the waterfall faucet.

"Do you…" She inhaled, feeling like it was going to be a week before she got enough oxygen again. "Do you think the neighbors heard?"

"I fucking hope so," Tracker said. "I want everyone to know you're mine."

She was. And after that, all of Madrid probably knew it too.

What a wonderful way to end a shitty day.

Chapter 20

Tracker held Stacey close as she slept. She felt good in his arms. She felt…right.

As a slave, he couldn't take a mate—at least, not in the traditional werewolf way that would form a supernatural bond. But Stacey was no less his. He'd claimed her last night in every way he could.

And it was possible that she was pregnant.

He tucked her even tighter against him. They hadn't talked about anything permanent beyond that, but a kid was pretty damned long term.

But would she change her mind when he told her that the nightmare wasn't over?

For her, it might be just beginning, and it was something that hadn't occurred to him until this morning.

She yawned and stretched, and then she wiggled around to face him, a smile on her kiss-swollen lips.

His little warrior.

"Hey, you," she murmured.

"Hey." He brushed his lips over hers and then nuzzled her neck in greeting. Felt so natural to be himself. To be a warg.

Her hand came up to cup his cheek, her thumb stroking lightly along his jaw. "What's the matter?"

"How do you know something's wrong?"

She frowned. "I don't know. I just do."

He didn't want to tell her, but she needed to know. Awkwardly, he sat up and swung his legs out of bed. "I'll make some coffee." They'd both need fortification for this.

Before he could stand, she grabbed his wrist. "Tell me."

He didn't look at her. Focused on a painting of a bull being tortured by some guy wearing ridiculously ornate, tight pants and holding a red flag. That was human art? He'd only seen cruelty like that in Sheoul. Maybe humans *were* as bad as he'd been taught.

"You're going to hate me."

"Tracker? After all we've been through, do you have so little faith in me?"

She was right. He hadn't thought of it that way. But her faith didn't make it any easier. Stomach churning, he shifted around to her.

"At some point during the battle…" He reached out and traced the mostly healed scratches on her shoulder and the scar-puckered punctures along her clavicle. "You were bitten and clawed. I'm sorry, Stacey. You…you're going to turn into a werewolf. And not like me. You'll be turned. *Vârcolac.* Out of control on the nights of the full moon."

"Oh, that." She contemplated what he'd said for about ten seconds, and then yawned again. "Meh. I'll deal. I'll have to chain myself three nights every month, but I get to live longer, so, you know, bonus. Plus, DART is cool with supes."

He was so stunned that all he could say was, "Supes?"

"Supernaturals." She propped herself up on one elbow. "Heck, I swear half of all DART members are some sort of demon, vampire, or shapeshifter. And the other half are married to demons, vampires, or shapeshifters. So it's all cool. I'm just glad I didn't volunteer for the werewolf vaccine trial."

"There's a werewolf vaccine trial?"

"Yeah. The people at Underworld General have been working on one. I think there's a vampire vaccine in the works too. Anyway, now that humans are aware of the existence of demons and such, there's a demand for it. The Aegis and DART are the first volunteers for the trials."

Tracker, as a werewolf, wasn't sure what to think about that. It was kind of insulting to be considered a disease that needed to be eradicated. But when he thought about how Stacey had been infected against her will, he got it. She seemed to be cool with it, but there were a lot of people who didn't feel the same.

It was definitely not a black and white issue.

Stacey was lucky though; as long as he was with her, she wouldn't need to chain herself. She could run with him, and he'd keep her out of trouble and away from humans. They could be together in both forms and in all the ways it mattered.

He was about to tell her that when the air next to the bed shimmered, and the next thing he knew, Harvester was standing there in a tight red leather minidress and stilettos with heels that looked like they were made to stake vampires.

"Good morning, sleepyheads." Her singsong voice carried through the room. "Hope I didn't interrupt anything. Looks like you just got started, so, you know, whew. Are you ready to go home?"

Stacey tugged the sheet up over her breasts and sat up. "Just let me wrap myself up in a towel. My clothes are ruined."

"Humans," Harvester sighed. "So modest. Hold on." She flashed out of there.

Stacey reached beneath the covers and grasped his shaft so firmly he gasped. "She thinks we were just getting started. Maybe we have time to finish."

"I like the way you think," he rasped, "but Harvester will be back—"

She popped into the room with an armful of clothes. "Here you go. I brought things for both of you. I'll go fetch some breakfast while you dress." She flashed back out.

Stacey stared at the empty air where Harvester had been. "Does she do that often? Just appear and disappear whenever she wants?"

"I don't know. I haven't seen her since she gave me the coin."

"Things were that bad with her, huh?"

He shrugged. "I didn't want to see her, and I doubt she wanted to see me, either. I'm sure I remind her of a time she'd rather forget."

"It sounds like your relationship with her is complicated."

"It is." But it was less complicated now than it had been. She'd saved Stacey's life, and for that, he would be forever grateful.

Stacey climbed out of bed, and he stifled a groan at the sight of her naked body. "I'm going to get dressed before she pops back in."

Yeah, he should do that too.

Stacey divvied up the clothes, which all had tags from Harrods. "Wow," she murmured as she held up a sky blue sweater with a five hundred dollar price tag. "Harvester doesn't mess around." She smoothed her hands over a pair of jeans. "I've never worn a three hundred dollar pair of pants before."

Tracker scowled at her clothes. "Are you sure the tag is real? Those jeans have holes in them. They look like they've been worn before. A lot."

She laughed. "It's called 'distressed.' They're supposed to look like that."

He looked at his own jeans, which didn't have holes. Secretly, he was glad. Seemed weird to pay so much for clothes that were already destroyed. And for some reason, his *not* distressed jeans cost less than hers.

Fashion was weird.

She handed him a big shoe box and opened up a much smaller one containing comfy-looking black flats with teal bottoms that made her squeal with delight. Why, he had no idea. Fashion baffled him *and* was weird.

That said, he had to give a low whistle of appreciation at the black leather biker boots with the thousand dollar price tag.

Whatever. They were comfortable, as was everything else. And he had to admit that the clothes looked amazing, as if they'd been tailored for them both.

That said, he planned to take Stacey out of her clothes as soon as possible. They'd look even better on the floor next to the bed.

Harvester materialized again with a bag of food from a French bakery. "Very nice," she said, giving them both an appreciative once-over.

Stacey smoothed her hands down the silky top. "Thank you, but seems kind of extravagant for a journey between the hotel room and Tracker's cabin that takes place in the blink of an eye and where no one will see us."

Harvester waved her hand in dismissal. "That's one of the bennies of being an angel. I can get whatever I want. Cost is not an issue." She looked at each of them in turn, obviously happy with her clothing choices. "Are you ready?"

Tracker took Stacey's hand, and they both nodded.

"Then let's take you home."

Home.

That sounded amazing.

* * * *

Stacey and Tracker arrived at Jillian's property at a little before ten A.M. After they scarfed down the croissant sandwiches Harvester brought, Tracker went to check on the animals while Stacey remained behind to call and check on her parents.

Unfortunately, she had to wait because Harvester didn't seem inclined to go anywhere, and Stacey figured it was rude to ask an angel to leave.

She still couldn't believe an actual angel was standing right in front of her. And dressed like *that.*

"Thank you for everything," she said, feeling a little awkward now that there was no emergency and Tracker wasn't around. How did one carry on a conversation with a Heavenly being who had once been a fallen angel? And who had once owned Tracker? Oh, and whose father was *the* Satan? "I will forever be in your debt."

"I owe Tracker far more than what little I've done. You won't be in my debt unless you harm him." She glanced down at her black-lacquered fingernails and said casually, "You won't do that, will you."

Stacey swallowed dryly. "I won't. Not ever."

Harvester's gaze narrowed. "Are you sure about that?"

Okay, this chick might be an all-powerful angel, but Stacey was starting to bristle at this line of questioning.

"After what you did to him for years," she said, "I'm surprised you have the gall to ask me that."

Harvester's eyes flickered in surprise. "And after you saw what I did to the werewolves who would have killed you, I'm surprised you have the gall to say that to *me*."

Truthfully, Stacey had surprised her own self. She should shut up right now, but hell, she'd gone this far, so why not go all the way? "Are you threatening me?"

Harvester's lips curved into a cruel smile, and Stacey could definitely see how she'd have excelled at being a fallen angel. "If I were threatening you," she said in a cold-ass voice that gave Stacey gooseflesh, "you'd already be preparing yourself to be a stain on the floor. No," she continued. "I'm making sure you're a worthy mate for Tracker."

Well, at least she had Tracker's well-being in mind. But still, Stacey wasn't sure what to think. "Look, I can't pretend to know anything about your past with him except for what he told me, and I'm sure there were a lot of extenuating circumstances, and as grateful as I am for your help..."

"You don't like me. It's okay," Harvester said with a shrug. "No one does. Apparently, I'm a bit abrasive." She wandered over to the front window and peered out before turning back to Stacey. "And I've done some horrible things. I mean, I did smash my mate under a mountain once. And I made Tracker help me cut off his wings and get him addicted to marrow wine. I tried to kill him a few times, too. But it all worked out in the end, didn't it?"

Um...

Stacey had no idea how to respond to that. Good thing Harvester continued talking.

"Anyway, assuming you two want to be together, Jillian will have the ability to transfer Tracker's bond to you, should he wish it."

Every drop of liquid evaporated out of Stacey's mouth. Harvester was suggesting that *Stacey* should be Tracker's owner? That she would *own* the man she loved?

"Oh, hell, no," she croaked.

"So you would prefer that another woman holds your man's leash?"

When she put it like that, Stacey wanted to scream. "Maybe it would be different if it were any other woman than Jillian, but it's not. Jillian wants only what's best for Tracker, and I trust her."

That seemed to satisfy the angel, and she nodded. "As do I. But if you change your mind, I can facilitate the transfer. I'll leave you now, but remember, if you hurt Tracker, you'll answer to me."

"And if you hurt him again, you'll answer to *me*." Stacey had no idea why she said that. It was stupid, given the massive power gap between them. But Harvester merely inclined her head in a respectful nod and flashed out of there.

Huh.

Once Stacey calmed down and got her jangled nerves under control, she called to check on her parents. They were fine, and they were happy to report that all the roads were now cleared and open.

The fact that it was fifty degrees and sunny was helping a lot too. Heck, it was supposed to be warm enough by midafternoon that she could probably sit on the front porch and enjoy the outdoors.

But what about tonight?

There were still two more full moons, and she wasn't sure if she was going to join Tracker in turning. She'd learned through her DART training that the lycanthropic disease sometimes didn't take full effect until the following month. In fact, if she called Kynan right now, the vaccine might even be effective in preventing it from happening at all.

She looked down at her phone. Calling would be the responsible thing to do, at least from a vaccine test standpoint. The researchers would give their left horns, or hooves, or whatever they had, in order to test its effectiveness in situations like hers.

But dammit, it was kind of…cool.

She was a fucking *werewolf.*

A couple of years ago, she'd have freaked out. Now she was excited. And, okay, maybe a little freaked out. This wasn't a drastically different haircut or nose job or a tattoo she'd have to hide from her parents.

This was a change of *species.* If she wasn't careful, she could actually *eat* a person.

So, yeah. Scary. She didn't even like *sushi.*

And how the hell *was* she going to tell her parents? They threatened to disown her for a *tattoo.* Maybe she shouldn't tell them. But her associates at DART would definitely have to know.

So would Jillian.

That made her laugh out loud.

Jillian was going to have a cow. About the werewolf thing, about how it had happened…about all of it, really.

Stacey remembered when she'd learned about the existence of the paranormal world and that Jillian was sleeping with the scariest Horseman of the Apocalypse. She'd actually passed out.

Telling Jillian about the werewolf thing might be fun. Payback, baby!

Grinning, she sent her friend a quick text.

Stacey: Hey, is Reseph back yet? Let's get together soon. So much to tell you!

Jillian texted back almost immediately. Stacey was pretty sure that when she wasn't gallivanting around the globe she was glued to her phone most days.

Jillian: He got back yesterday! He's sleeping like the dead right now, but as soon as he wakes up, I'll have him gate me there.

Stacey: Just keep in mind that it's a full moon tonight, so don't come if it's after dark.

Jillian: Why not? Tracker can chain himself up and we can talk. It'll be fine.

It wouldn't be fine if Stacey turned into a werewolf and attacked her. But now wasn't the time to tell Jillian the truth. Not in a text.

Stacey: I just think he'd like to see you.
Jillian: Real*ly?*
Jillian: Okay. We'll come this afternoon.
Stacey: Awesome. See you soon!
Stacey put down the phone. This was going to be a blast.

Chapter 21

Evie didn't leave Rick's side even once during the two hours Tracker spent working in the barn. Rick didn't seem too traumatized by his ordeal, but even the donkeys were extra clingy when Tracker released them all into the outdoor pen while he cleaned their stalls and feeders.

When he was done, he gave them their food, plus an extra treat to help make up for all the shit they'd gone through over the last couple of days.

He also told them that the scumbags who had taken Rick were dead, and while they didn't understand, he felt better saying it.

Who knew that talking could be such a freeing thing? After a lifetime of being afraid to speak, he was just starting to understand the power of conversation. The things Stacey had shared with him had expanded his world, and what he'd shared with her had freed him in all ways but one.

And that one…it was a fucking doozie.

He was still a slave, and they were going to have to deal with it. They were going to have to find a way to have a relationship that involved a third person.

Unless Stacey would agree to take his bond.

Taking a deep, bracing breath ahead of the talk they were about to have, he walked through the front door and into a cabin filled with the savory aroma of beef, onions, and baking bread.

His mouth watered, but it was as much a reaction to the food as it was the fact that she was wearing skin-tight black leggings and a blue T-shirt of his that didn't hide the definition in her firm buttocks.

"Hey." Stacey looked over her shoulder at him from where she was rinsing dishes at the kitchen sink. "The pork chops you bought were spoiled from being left out, so I thought I'd make some homemade stew and bread. Are you hungry?"

His stomach growled as if fighting for dominance in the battle between his two hungers.

He didn't bother taking off his boots before clomping across the floor, tracking snow. "Starving." He bent over and nuzzled his way through her hair to her neck. He kissed her there, lingering on one of the scars she'd taken in the battle. "*Really* starving."

"Mmm." Reaching up, she slid her wet, soapy hand along his jaw. "It'll be ready in ten minutes. Enough time for a quickie."

If "quickie" meant sex, he was in.

"Want to join me in the shower?" he murmured in her ear, and she nodded.

"Just let me finish up here."

"I'll get the water running." He started for the bedroom but paused at the threshold. "Thank you, Stacey."

"For what?"

He wasn't sure how to say what he was feeling, and it took him a second to gather his thoughts. "For making this cabin feel like a home. Always before, it was a place to live."

"Tracker…" Stacey took a deep breath and moved toward him. "I don't know what it is, but I've always felt a connection to you. And now with the werewolf thing, it's even stronger. Do you feel the same way? Or is this one sided."

"No," he said in a rush. "It's not one sided. I've wanted you for a long time, but I didn't think I could have you. I never thought I could have…" He made an encompassing gesture around the cabin. "This. A home of my own. A female of my own. A *life* of my own. You changed everything." He took a deep breath. "There's just one thing that could make it better."

"What's that?"

Say it. Just say it. "Will you take my bond?"

Every drop of color drained from Stacey's face. "Did you just…you didn't really ask that. Right?"

"I wouldn't ask if it weren't important."

The sound of bubbling stew seemed unnaturally loud as Stacey looked over at the pot, a dish towel clenched in her hands. "Did Harvester say something to you?"

"Why would Harvester say anything to me about this?"

"Because she tried to talk me into taking your bond."

Harvester had done that? For him? "What did you say?"

"I said no." She wrung the towel in her hands as she spoke, her gaze locked on it. "I can't own you. How is a relationship fair or equal if one person has that much power?"

"You would rather Jillian have that power? Do you understand that if she's ever in trouble, I'm compelled to go to her? I would have to leave *you* to go to her."

"If that's the case, then clearly she needs you."

"Dammit, Stacey, she has Reseph. What happens if *you* need me?" He crossed to her in three strides, seized her by the shoulders, and kissed her hard. "I love you, female. You already own my heart. Why not the rest of me?"

Tears welled in her eyes, and he suddenly felt like shit. He was asking her to do something that would make her miserable, that went against her very nature.

He'd spent over sixty years in misery, and he couldn't resign her to the same fate.

"It's okay," he said softly. "I take it back—"

They both jumped at the sound of a knock at the door.

"Must be Jillian." Stacey swallowed, dabbed at her eyes with the towel. "I'm going to tell her it's a bad time."

She reached for the door, and as her fingers closed around the knob, a sense of evil nearly took him to his knees. Terror froze his feet to the floor, and he tried to warn her, but nothing would come out of his mouth.

She whipped open the door and gasped.

Standing there, filling the doorway, was a seven-foot tall Neethul demon, his platinum hair draped over his broad shoulders, his elfin ears poking through.

Like all of his species, he was beautiful. Deceptively beautiful.

Tracker knew he was hideous inside.

The male standing there with a whip in one hand and restraints in the other was the thing that haunted Tracker's dreams and paralyzed him with fear like nothing else could.

A Neethul slaver.

Chapter 22

"Get away from the door," Tracker croaked.

Stacey did one better than that. She slammed the door, locked it, and then grabbed the ax propped against the wall. But as she hefted it up, the lock clicked and the door swung open with a whisper of evil magic.

Tracker didn't think. He simply moved, whipping Stacey behind him as he swept up the hatchet that had been next to the ax.

The slaver stepped inside with a hiss, and the door banged shut behind him.

"You know better than that, Whine." His hand came up, and with it, searing pain shot through every nerve in Tracker's body.

"My name," he ground out as he doubled over, "is Tracker."

"We no longer recognize your birth name," the slaver said. "Your *human* master had no right to give it back to you. Had we known of her violation, we'd have taken you from her immediately. You will be known as Whine from here on out."

Tracker suppressed a shudder. He'd been called a lot of names by a lot of masters, and ultimately, Whine wasn't the worst. But it was a reminder of a time best forgotten.

The slaver took a step closer. "Assume the position." When Tracker refused to budge, the demon's mouth twisted into a fangy snarl. "*On your knees, slave.*"

Tracker allowed himself a grim smile of defiance. He used to drop instantly at the command to assume the slave position, but over the last few years he'd tasted freedom. Independence. Kindness. He didn't want to go back. Didn't want the humiliation, especially not in front of Stacey.

"Fuck you," he murmured under his breath.

The slaver roared in fury and raised his whip. "*On. Your. Knees.*"

"Stop it!" Stacey cried as she rushed the bastard.

"No! Stacey, don't." Tracker moved to block her. The slaver would beat her at best, kill her at worst. He would rather go back to the life he hated than see Stacey die. Besides, he had Harvester's word. He wouldn't suffer long.

He dropped to his knees as ordered, hatred burning in every cell. He bowed his head and shot her a sideways glance. "Stay back. No matter what happens, stay back."

The slaver stepped behind him and, in a smooth, practiced motion, he fitted the spiky gag inside Tracker's mouth, secured it like a horse's bridle around his head, and then pulled the leather straps over his shoulders to secure his wrists behind his back. In this position, Tracker couldn't move a muscle without tearing his tongue, cheeks, and roof of his mouth to shreds.

"Why are you doing this?" Stacey demanded, tears glistening in her eyes.

"I need to speak to his owner. This is the summoning position."

"He couldn't have just kneeled? You had to restrain him?"

"It's how this business is conducted and the only way a human owner will sense her slave. Now, fuck off, maggot."

"I'm not going anywhere. I want to be here when Jillian arrives. You have no idea who she's m—"

Tracker shook his head, just barely, but it was still enough for a couple of spikes to jab into his flesh. Stacey looked at him, confused, but he just stared, telling her with his eyes to keep quiet. The demon was clearly not aware that Jillian was mated to one of the most powerful beings in existence, and Tracker didn't want him to know. Not until it was too late. No sense in letting the guy prepare or call for backup.

Tracker couldn't see the Neethul, but he could sense the demon's annoyance.

"Leave," he pleaded, the word mushy as he tried to speak around the spiked gag. Even that one word punctured his mouth in at least a half dozen places, and the metallic tang of blood tingled on his pierced tongue.

Stacey backed away, the pity and tears in her eyes punching him in the gut. He expected her to go outside, but she simply moved to the corner near the door, never taking her angry gaze off the demon, her fingers still wrapped tight around the ax handle.

Apparently satisfied, the slaver reached out and petted Tracker's head as he walked in a slow circle around him. "Your current master has been too permissive with you. She's spoiled you. Such a shame. It's why humans aren't usually allowed to own slaves. I will address this issue with the Council." He glanced at his watch. "She should be here soon."

Blood trickled out of Tracker's mouth and dripped down his chin. The soft plop of drops on the hardwood floor echoed through the cabin more loudly than it should have. But still, through the crackle of the fire in the wood stove and drip-drip of his blood, he heard the crunch of footsteps in the snow outside.

Jillian.

He smiled, even though two spikes punched into his lips. She wouldn't be here alone.

"Tracker?" She tapped on the door even though it was well within her rights to open it with no notice.

Stacey opened the door, Tracker's angle barely allowing him to see Jillian in the doorway.

"Stacey, hey. Is Tracker okay? I'm feeling weird—" Her gasp filled the room as she took in Tracker kneeling on the floor and the slaver standing next to him.

"Human," the guy rumbled. "We need to talk about your slave."

Slowly, deliberately, Jillian masked her fear and stepped inside, closing the door behind her. "Do we."

"You have committed several offenses, and I am hereby reclaiming this slave."

"I see." Jillian hefted her purse on her shoulder as if she was calmly haggling with a merchant at a market. "Why don't you tell me what these offenses are."

"He is not allowed to be known by his birth name. His birth name is considered property, and it is illegal for slaves to own property. It has also come to our attention that this hovel and farm are his."

She crossed her arms across her chest. "They are." She looked over at Tracker. "I was going to surprise you. I transferred both cabins and the property to you. I also bought back the three hundred acres my parents sold before they died."

Warmth flooded his body at her confession. He'd never so much as dreamed of owning a square foot of property, let alone five hundred acres and two houses.

But if the slavers had their way, he wouldn't be able to use any of it. Hell, he'd never see the land again. He doubted he'd ever even step foot in the human realm.

"He must be punished."

"What?" Stacey's hand clenched so tightly around the ax handle that her knuckles turned white. "It's not his fault. Jillian, can you transfer it back into your name?"

"No," she said. "I'm not going to do that. And Tracker isn't going to be punished."

"Stupid human," the slaver said. "You should never have held his bond. Had we known Harvester transferred him to you, we'd have corrected this error long ago." He reached into his bag and pulled out a small black disk. "I'm taking his bond back. After he's been punished, he'll be sold to another master."

"Me." Stacey moved closer to Tracker. "Give me the bond."

"No," he croaked, the word mushy, spoken through shredded flesh and blood.

The Neethul snorted. "Fool. I just said that humans can't—"

"I'm not human. Not anymore." She tugged down her shirt collar to reveal the scarred gouges from the battle. "I'm a werewolf."

"What?" Jillian pivoted to Stacey. "When? How?"

"Long story. I promise to tell you later." She looked down at Tracker. "I'll take it." When he shook his head at her, she smiled. "It's okay. It's not going to be easy, but we'll figure it out. Jillian..." She took a deep breath and turned to his master. "You didn't have a choice when you were given Tracker. It would be so selfish of me to make you bear that burden any longer."

The Neethul bared his fangs. "No one is taking his bond but me." He held out the disk to Jillian. "Touch it, human. Transfer the bond."

Jillian smiled, the fakest smile Tracker had ever seen. "I don't think so."

Baring his teeth, the Neethul drew a wicked blade from his hip sheathe. "You *will* transfer the bond."

"Let's try this again." She opened the door, letting in a blast of frigid air. "Get the hell out."

"You know I can kill you and take the bond."

"Try it, asshole."

The Neethul roared as he charged.

Jillian, moving like a wraith, darted outside, barely escaping the

Neethul's claws. And then Stacey was there, swinging the ax. The thud as it embedded deep into the demon's armored back rang out. The demon didn't miss a step, spinning around to grip Stacey by the throat.

Instant, hot fury boiled over in Tracker's veins. He didn't care about his pain. He didn't care about anything except making sure Jillian and Stacey stayed safe. He couldn't get to his feet, but he managed to leap through the door and bash the demon with his shoulder.

Blood poured out of his mouth as the spikes did their job, mangling his tongue, lips, and palate. But it was all worth it as the Neethul dropped Stacey and tumbled down the porch steps.

Tracker lay on the deck, unable to move as he watched the demon leap to his feet with a snarl. The whip in his hand uncoiled and lit with blue fire.

"Human bitches," he spat at Jillian and Stacey. "You're going to be our newest slaves."

* * * *

The air crackled as the demon raised his whip.

Fuck that. Stacey hadn't just survived werewolves to be enslaved. She caught Tracker's eye, and then she rushed the Neethul as Tracker kicked out.

Tracker's pain must have been unbearable as his boots cracked into the backs of the demon's knees. The slaver went down, flat on his back. Then, just like in old times dealing with bullies, Jillian and Stacey rushed him together. Jillian went for the whip, while Stacey smashed his face with her boot.

Tag team.

But the voice that rang out halted them both.

"Touch either of them, slaver, and I will shove that whip so far up your ass you'll be able to floss with it."

Reseph glanced apologetically at Jillian. "I hope it's okay that I barged in. I know you like to handle things like this yourself."

"Totally okay, baby," Jillian said, and Stacey was super cool with it, too.

The demon asshole staggered to his feet and glared at Reseph, who stood a few yards away, his hands tucked into his jeans pockets like this was no big deal. "Who the fuck are you?"

"Oh, so you didn't do your research about me?" Jillian said. "You know I'm human and that I gave Tracker property, but not who I'm mated to?"

He hissed. "I don't care."

Reseph beamed with pride as Jillian stepped forward. "I think you will." She gestured at her mate. "This is Reseph. And you're going to give him that disc."

The demon looked unimpressed. He practically yawned. "Who?"

"You might know him as Pestilence, first Horseman of the Apocalypse."

Reseph nodded pleasantly. "'Sup." With a flick of his finger against the crescent-shaped scar on his throat, plate metal armor folded into place, making him even more impressive than he already was.

It took a moment for the information to sink in, but once it did, the demon's eyes shot wide and he dropped to his knees, head bowed. "My Lord," he breathed. "It is an honor—"

"Save it, slime," Reseph said. "Give me the disc."

The guy's head popped up. "I cannot."

Reseph sighed, and then, from out of nowhere, he was holding a bow and arrow, the arrow pointed at the top of the demon's head.

"Pretty sure you can."

The demon swallowed. Hard. His hand shook as he held out the item. Reseph lowered his bow and took it in his big palm. "What is it?"

"They wanted me to transfer my bond with Tracker to it," Jillian said. "I'm thinking that if we lock it away someplace safe, they can never control him again."

"Reseph." Stacey grabbed the demon's belt, figuring the keys to Tracker's restraints might be in it. "Destroying it might break the slave bond. I remember something from one of my training manuals. That most powerful spells have to be grounded in an object. If that object is broken…"

"So is the spell." Reseph smiled at the slaver. "Is that true? Is this your dirty little secret of the 'unbreakable' bond."

The demon looked away, jaw tight.

Reseph moved in a blur, and the demon screamed, an arrow protruding from the crook of his neck and shoulder.

Reseph did not mess around.

"I have an unlimited number of arrows, shitbag."

The demon spoke through clenched teeth. "If the disc is broken, so is the slave bond."

"Sick." In one smooth motion, Reseph tossed the disc into the air, whipped up his bow, and fired a single shot. The arrow struck the little circle and shattered it into a million pieces.

Instantly, the harness that bound Tracker disintegrated into ash and blew away with the breeze. He fell forward, catching himself on two trembling arms.

"I'm free," he breathed. "I'm…free."

"Tracker!" Stacey rushed to him as Reseph seized the demon by his collar and hauled him off the ground.

"Now," he growled, "we're going to the slaver guild and getting Tracker some justice for the hell you've put him through."

The Horseman opened a gate and, with the slaver in his clutches, he stepped through it and disappeared.

Chapter 23

Tracker couldn't believe it.

Was afraid to believe it. Because what if it wasn't true?

But he couldn't deny that the ever-present tightness in the depths of his chest had melted away, and the heaviness that had always weighted him down was gone.

Still on his hands and knees, blood streaming down his chin, he glanced over at Jillian, who clutched her chest and stared at him in disbelief. He knew what she was feeling, because he felt it too.

Nothing.

The tether that wrapped around his heart like razor wire, the tether that had kept him leashed to her, and every master before her, no longer existed.

A great burden and sense of evil was gone.

He was free.

His unending nightmare had ended.

"Is it true?" Stacey knelt beside him in the snow, holding his head against her chest and stroking his hair. "Are you free?"

Unable to find his voice, he nodded. Jillian grinned at him, tears streaming down her cheeks.

"I'm so happy for you, Tracker. I'm so happy for all of us." She came over and kneeled down, bringing them all into a group hug. "Whatever you guys need, you just let us know, okay?"

"Thank you," Stacey said in a voice thick with emotion. "I guess…right now I could use your help getting him inside."

"I'mna uh inalid." He spit blood and tried that again. "I'm not an invalid." He was just coming to grips with a dream coming true.

"I'm thinking a trip to Underworld General would be a good idea," Jillian said as he lurched to his feet. "Your mouth is pretty torn up."

He shook his head. A nap would heal him most of the way, and tonight's moon shift would heal the rest.

"Yo!"

They all wheeled around at the deep voice belonging to Reseph's brother Thanatos. He stepped out of his gate with a dark-haired male in black scrubs. Tracker had seen Eidolon a couple times before when Reseph and Jillian hosted parties.

Jillian smiled and waved. "Did Reseph send you?"

Thanatos nodded, the blond braids at his temples swinging against his cheeks. "Fortunately, the doc wasn't busy."

Eidolon scowled at the Horseman as he came over to Tracker. "I was at *work*. You basically kidnapped me."

"Please. You were in your office, dicking around at your computer." Thanatos gestured to Tracker. "Look. Blood. This is medical shit. You know, your *work*, Doctor. And hurry. I have places to be and people to kill."

Eidolon heaved a sigh and clamped his hand down on Tracker's shoulder. "I'm uninviting you to our next Christmas party. And you, Tracker, are going to feel a tingle."

The black glyphs running from the tips of Eidolon's fingers to the base of his jaw lit up, and as Thanatos and Eidolon gave each other shit, Tracker surrendered to the healing vibrations flowing from the demon who ran Underworld General.

Within seconds, the pain eased as his flesh knit together, cycling down into what ended up being only the dullest ache in his jaw.

"There." Eidolon stepped back. "Besides the mouth trauma, you had a lot of damaged organs." Sympathy swirled in the doctor's dark eyes. "You've been through a lot. I healed what I could. Oh, and I know slaves are rendered infertile through the bond, but you should know that you are now fully functional."

Tracker swallowed. He could have kids. If Stacey wasn't pregnant after last night, it wouldn't be a total tragedy. He and Stacey could have young later, when they were ready.

"He was fully functional last night," Stacey said, and all eyes fixed on her. Pink splotches broke out on her cheeks when she realized what she'd said. "What? He was. He'd been injected with sex demon stuff."

Eidolon swung back around to Tracker. "What was that?"

"A demon injected me with Seminus serum…or something like that. Said it would make me temporarily fertile. Made me so fucked up." He eyed Eidolon with pity. "I feel for you."

"Interesting. I want to talk to you later about that." Eidolon turned to Stacey. "Do you need to know if you're pregnant?"

"Ah…well, yes, but I can just get a test at the store…"

He gripped her shoulder, and his arm lit up again. After a moment he dropped his hand. "Do you want to know now?"

Stacey glanced at Tracker, and they both nodded.

Eidolon shoved his hands in his pockets. "You're not."

Tracker was okay with that, but he'd have been okay if it had gone the other way too, and Stacey's reassuring nod said the same thing.

"Also," Eidolon continued, "you've been infected with the lycanthropic virus. I can send someone with a dose of the vaccine—"

"No. Thank you, but I think I'm going to pass."

Eidolon's eyes flickered in surprise, then his expression became one of respect and approval. "If you change your mind, you probably have until the next moon cycle to decide. Right now it's a light viral load, so you probably won't shift tonight or tomorrow. Just FYI."

"Thank you, Doctor," Tracker said. He squeezed Stacey's hand. "I'm ready for that stew."

As far as hints went, it wasn't the most subtle, but he really was hungry, and he wanted to celebrate.

Maybe Stacey could make margaritas again, too.

"Wait." Jillian blocked their path. "I know you're going to hate this idea, but I want to have a party the day after tomorrow, after the third moon shift. Here. To celebrate Tracker's freedom." She tapped Stacey playfully on the shoulder. "And your induction into the World of the Weird."

A party? With a whole bunch of people?

Jillian was right. His first instinct was to tell her no. He wasn't comfortable with people. With attention.

But that was the result of decades of living in fear. It was time to shed the past, make new memories, and embrace his new life.

"Thank you, mistr—" He stopped himself, took a deep breath, and forced his lips to address her in a way he thought would never happen. "Thank you…Jillian." Happy tears welled in her eyes, and Stacey's too, and his sense of freedom expanded even more. He felt whole. Healed. Ready to party. Later. "Let's do it. But tonight, I just want some stew."

Their laughter followed him and Stacey up the steps to the porch and into the cabin.

"Well," Stacey said as she headed for the kitchen. "This has been an interesting day."

He remained where he was, watching her, humbled by her resilience. After everything she'd been through, she was still a bundle of positive energy.

"You would have taken the bond for me," he said, and she came to a dead stop.

Very slowly, she turned around, the steely gray in her eyes turning misty. "For *us*. It would have been hard, but no more difficult than what you and Jillian were already living with. It would have been a very small sacrifice in the grand scheme of things." She came back to him. "I mean, you would have gone with the slaver to save me."

"I would suffer a hundred more masters if it meant keeping you safe."

She looked up at him with so much tenderness that it actually hurt. "I couldn't have lived with that, Tracker."

Moisture stung his eyes. "Well, we don't have to worry about it anymore. We don't have to worry about anything."

He took a deep, cleansing breath, savoring the sensation of being unburdened by his slave bond.

Everything he did for the rest of the day…shower, eat, drink, make love to Stacey…everything was like new. Fresh.

Clean.

And with the clean start, came new ideas and so many more possibilities. He was running a zillion of them through his head after a marathon couple of hours of lovemaking when Stacey snuggled up to him in bed just as the sun was beginning to set.

"What are you thinking?"

"That I need to get dressed."

"Why?" She trailed her fingernails down his chest as she lay in the crook of his arm. "Don't you usually chain yourself up naked?"

"I'm not chaining myself tonight," Tracker said. "Tonight, I'm going to claim what's mine."

Stacey propped herself up on one elbow and gave him a flirty smile. "Do you mean me?"

The heat in her gaze made his cock twitch, but he didn't have time for that. The full moon was on its way. "I've already claimed you," he purred. "You're mine now."

"Yes," she whispered, "I am."

He kissed her, pouring everything he had into it. When he was done, they were both panting and groping and he figured he could spare a *little* time. But before they went there, he continued.

"I'm going to claim the pack. If you shift with me, we'll go together."

She somehow looked both excited and wary. "How many are left?"

"The ones who chained themselves or who refused to join in the hunt. All who stood with Victoria are dead. Those who remain are doomed to die without someone of my blood leading them."

"So you're going to save them?"

"I am. Tonight," he said as he reached for her. "I will claim my pack, and shit is going to change."

Chapter 24

Stacey sat with Jillian next to the bonfire, a pitcher of margaritas on the patio table between them. She was disappointed that for the last two nights Tracker had shifted into his beast form while she'd remained in her boring old human body, but with every refill of her glass, she got more over it.

But next month? She was so running with her mate instead of watching him take off to assume control of what remained of his pack. At some point, he would move them here, but for now she and Tracker would enjoy their time alone.

"I am so happy for you, Stacey," Jillian said as she put her glass down. "I mean, the werewolf thing is going to take a little getting used to, but at least I know you're going to be around for a long time."

Stacey leaned back in her folding chair with a lazy grin. "I love that my lifespan quadrupled. So awesome."

"Have you told your bosses at DART yet?"

"Yep. And they're totally cool with it." She swiped salt off the rim of her glass with her tongue because she knew Tracker was watching. He was working on his social skills with Ares over by the barn, but she felt his hot gaze every so often. Like now. "I've probably become an even bigger asset to them."

"What about your parents?"

"My extremely religious Mom and Dad who don't read or watch anything that's not in line with Biblical teachings? Yeah…no. I don't even wear leggings to their house. I'm not telling them I've been turned into a creature whose origins are in Hell."

Jillian laughed. "Probably smart." She glanced over at her own mate, who was getting ready to go country karaoke on the stage he and his brothers had built for the party next to the barn. Inside, they'd strung lights and cleared space for a dance floor…they'd even arranged for all of the Seminus demon families to come over and have barbecue and beer around the three bonfires. "You have a brand new life now."

"So do a whole lot of people, thanks to them."

Jillian nodded. "I can't believe they took out a major slave operation."

Neither could Stacey. Apparently, Reseph had taken the slaver to Ares's Greek palace, where he'd gathered his siblings and launched an assault on the slaver's organization, which turned out to be the largest in all the realms. They'd killed dozens of Neethul slave traders and released hundreds of slaves, many of whom had been in such bad condition that they'd been admitted to UGH. Then, after everyone was dead or rescued, the Horsemen had raided the organization's coffers and bank accounts and distributed the funds to the victims. Tracker had received millions in compensation for his years as a slave.

Because slavery was legal in Sheoul, what they'd all done constituted a crime, but no one was going to mess with the Four Horsemen of the Apocalypse, especially since the current king of Hell was their former Watcher.

And their uncle.

Jillian took a long sip of her margarita. "It's weird, isn't it, how we both found our mates in a blizzard?"

Stacey snorted. "The difference being that I knew Tracker before holing up with him in a storm. You were trapped with some strange guy who could have been a dangerous maniac for all you knew. Oh, and guess what? It turns out that he *was* a dangerous maniac."

Jillian laughed. "Yeah, but did you threaten your man with a frying pan?"

"Didn't need to," Stacey shot back, and then waggled her brows. "Did you get busy in the barn?"

"Obviously."

Okay, Stacey needed to get ahead in the game. "Did you get kidnapped by ravenous werewolves and have to fight your way out?"

"Hmm." Jillian made a show of thinking about that. "No, but I did nearly get killed by Lucifer."

Stacey rolled her eyes. "Okay, I give up. You win the craziest *how did you meet* competition."

They both laughed, and as they caught each other's eye, the air around them stilled, its energy shifting.

"I'm glad everything worked out for you and Tracker." Jillian fiddled with the base of her glass. "I'm really sorry if I wasn't supportive at first."

There was no need for an apology. "You were just reacting to my negativity. I think I'd been feeling kind of left out, you know? You had this whole new life I didn't understand and wasn't part of. I felt like we were drifting apart. You're too important to me to let that happen."

Now, for the first time in a long time, they had things in common again. Heck, now that she thought about it, maybe joining DART had even been a way to connect not just with Jillian, but with the outside world that seemed to be leaving her and her little Colorado town behind.

Smiling, Jillian reached out and gave Stacey's hand a gentle squeeze. "Same. I'm so happy for both of us. I wouldn't change a thing."

Stacey looked over at Reseph, where he was testing the mic. He was hot, and he could sing, she'd give him that. Smart, powerful, and funny. Definitely too arrogant for his own good. Stacey used to be envious of her friend, who had gotten it all when she hooked up with her dream man.

But then she thought about Tracker, about his strength of character, and how her mom had once said that the strongest people were those who fell the furthest and struggled the hardest to climb out of the darkest pits.

She thought about how he'd assumed the lead in his pack, and he'd promised them fairness and progress, and he wanted her to help.

She was going to be a freaking pack leader. And DART was cool with that. Holy crap!

So, yeah, Jillian had it all, but Stacey wasn't jealous anymore. Not one bit.

Because she had it all too.

Still, she couldn't resist a little jab. "Oh, hey, Jillian. I'm a werewolf and you're not."

Her friend tore her gaze away from her mate. "What was that?"

"Nothing." Stacey shrugged and hid her smile in her margarita. "Absolutely nothing."

* * * *

Also from 1001 Dark Nights and Larissa Ione, discover Reaper, Cipher, Dining With Angels, Her Guardian Angel, Hawkyn, Razr, Hades, Z, and Azagoth.

Discover 1001 Dark Nights Collection Eight

DRAGON REVEALED by Donna Grant
A Dragon Kings Novella

CAPTURED IN INK by Carrie Ann Ryan
A Montgomery Ink: Boulder Novella

SECURING JANE by Susan Stoker
A SEAL of Protection: Legacy Series Novella

WILD WIND by Kristen Ashley
A Chaos Novella

DARE TO TEASE by Carly Phillips
A Dare Nation Novella

VAMPIRE by Rebecca Zanetti
A Dark Protectors/Rebels Novella

MAFIA KING by Rachel Van Dyken
A Mafia Royals Novella

THE GRAVEDIGGER'S SON by Darynda Jones
A Charley Davidson Novella

FINALE by Skye Warren
A North Security Novella

MEMORIES OF YOU by J. Kenner
A Stark Securities Novella

SLAYED BY DARKNESS by Alexandra Ivy
A Guardians of Eternity Novella

TREASURED by Lexi Blake
A Masters and Mercenaries Novella

THE DAREDEVIL by Dylan Allen
A Rivers Wilde Novella

BOND OF DESTINY by Larissa Ione
A Demonica Novella

THE CLOSE-UP by Kennedy Ryan
A Hollywood Renaissance Novella

MORE THAN POSSESS YOU by Shayla Black
A More Than Words Novella

HAUNTED HOUSE by Heather Graham
A Krewe of Hunters Novella

MAN FOR ME by Laurelin Paige
A Man In Charge Novella

THE RHYTHM METHOD by Kylie Scott
A Stage Dive Novella

JONAH BENNETT by Tijan
A Bennett Mafia Novella

CHANGE WITH ME by Kristen Proby
A With Me In Seattle Novella

THE DARKEST DESTINY by Gena Showalter
A Lords of the Underworld Novella

Also from Blue Box Press

THE LAST TIARA by M.J. Rose

THE CROWN OF GILDED BONES by Jennifer L. Armentrout
A Blood and Ash Novel

THE MISSING SISTER by Lucinda Riley

THE END OF FOREVER by Steve Berry and M.J. Rose
A Cassiopeia Vitt Adventure

THE STEAL by C. W. Gortner and M.J. Rose

CHASING SERENITY by Kristen Ashley
A River Rain Novel

A SHADOW IN THE EMBER by Jennifer L. Armentrout
A Flesh and Fire Novel

Discover More Larissa Ione

Reaper: A Demonica Novel
By Larissa Ione

He is the Keeper of Souls. Judge, jury, and executioner. He is death personified.

He is the Grim Reaper.

A fallen angel who commands the respect of both Heaven and Hell, Azagoth has presided over his own underworld realm for thousands of years. As the overlord of evil souls, he maintains balance crucial to the existence of life on Earth and beyond. But as all the realms gear up for the prophesied End of Days, the ties that bind him to Sheoul-gra have begun to chafe.

Now, with his beloved mate and unborn child the target of an ancient enemy, Azagoth will stop at nothing to save them, even if it means breaking blood oaths and shattering age-old alliances.

Even if it means destroying himself and setting the world on fire…

* * * *

Hawkyn: A Demonica Novella
By Larissa Ione

As a special class of earthbound guardian angel called Memitim, Hawkyn is charged with protecting those whose lives are woven into the fabric of the future. His success is legendary, so when he's given a serial killer to watch over, he sees no reason for that to change. But Hawkyn's own future is jeopardized after he breaks the rules and rescues a beautiful woman from the killer's clutches, setting off an explosive, demonic game of cat and mouse that pits brother against brother and that won't end until someone dies.

Aurora Mercer is the half-wytch lone survivor of a psychopath who gets off on the sadistic torture of his victims. A psychopath whose obsessive psyche won't let him move on until he kills her. Now she's marked for death, her fate tied to that of a murderer...and to a sexy angel who makes her blood burn with desire...

* * * *

Cipher: A Demonica Underworld Novella
By Larissa Ione

It's been seven months since Cipher, an Unfallen angel who straddled a razor thin line between good and evil, woke up in hell with a new set of wings, a wicked pair of fangs, and a handler who's as beautiful as she is dangerous. As a laid-back cyber-specialist who once assisted guardian angels, he'd been in a prime position to earn back his halo. But now, as a True Fallen forced to use his talents for malevolence, he must fight not only his captors and his sexy handler, but the growing corruption inside him...before the friends searching for him become his enemies and he becomes his own worst nightmare.

Lyre is a fallen angel with a heart full of hate. When she's assigned to ensure that Cipher carries out their boss's orders, she sees an opportunity to take revenge on those who wronged her. All she has to do is appeal to Cipher's burgeoning dark side. But the devastatingly handsome fellow True Fallen has other ideas — sexy ideas that threaten to derail all Lyre's plans and put them in the path of an approaching hell storm.

Danger and desire explode, even as Cipher and Lyre unravel a sinister plot that will fracture the underworld and send shockwaves into Heaven itself...

* * * *

Dining with Angels: Bits & Bites from the Demonica Universe
by Larissa Ione, Recipes by Suzanne M. Johnson

In a world where humans and supernatural beings coexist — not always peacefully — three things can bring everyone to the table: Love, a mutual enemy, and, of course, food.

With seven brand new stories from the Demonica universe, New

York Times bestselling author Larissa Ione has the love and enemies covered, while celebrity Southern food expert Suzanne Johnson brings delicious food to the party.

And who doesn't love a party? (Harvester rolls her eyes and raises her hand, but we know she's lying.)

Join Ares and Cara as they celebrate a new addition to their family. See what Reaver and Harvester are doing to "spice" things up. Find out what trouble Reseph might have gotten himself into with Jillian. You'll love reading about the further adventures of Wraith and Serena, Declan and Suzanne, and Shade and Runa, and you're not going to want to miss the sit down with Eidolon and Tayla.

So pour a glass of the Grim Reaper's finest wine and settle in for slices of life from your favorite characters and the recipes that bring them together. Whether you're dining with angels, drinking with demons, or hanging with humans, you'll find the perfect heavenly bits and sinful bites to suit the occasion.

Happy reading and happy eating!

* * * *

Her Guardian Angel: A Demonica Underworld/Masters and Mercenaries Novella

by Larissa Ione

After a difficult childhood and a turbulent stint in the military, Declan Burke finally got his act together. Now he's a battle-hardened professional bodyguard who takes his job at McKay-Taggart seriously and his playtime – and his play*mates* – just as seriously. One thing he never does, however, is mix business with pleasure. But when the mysterious, gorgeous Suzanne D'Angelo needs his protection from a stalker, his desire for her burns out of control, tempting him to break all the rules…even as he's drawn into a dark, dangerous world he didn't know existed.

Suzanne is an earthbound angel on her critical first mission: protecting Declan from an emerging supernatural threat at all costs. To keep him close, she hires him as her bodyguard. It doesn't take long for her to realize that she's in over her head, defenseless against this devastatingly sexy human who makes her crave his forbidden touch.

Together they'll have to draw on every ounce of their collective training to resist each other as the enemy closes in, but soon it becomes apparent that nothing could have prepared them for the menace to their lives…or their hearts.

* * * *

Razr: A Demonica Underworld Novella

by Larissa Ione

A fallen angel with a secret.

An otherworldly elf with an insatiable hunger she doesn't understand.

An enchanted gem.

Meet mortal enemies Razr and Jedda...and the priceless diamond that threatens to destroy them both even as it bonds them together with sizzling passion.

Welcome back to the Demonica Underworld, where enemies find love...if they're strong enough to survive.

* * * *

Z: A Demonica Underworld Novella

by Larissa Ione

Zhubaal, fallen angel assistant to the Grim Reaper, has spent decades searching for the angel he loved and lost nearly a century ago. Not even her death can keep him from trying to find her, not when he knows she's been given a second chance at life in a new body. But as time passes, he's losing hope, and he wonders how much longer he can hold to the oath he swore to her so long ago…

As an *emim*, the wingless offspring of two fallen angels, Vex has always felt like a second-class citizen. But if she manages to secure a deal with the Grim Reaper — by any means necessary — she will have earned her place in the world. The only obstacle in the way of her plan is a sexy hardass called Z, who seems determined to thwart her at every turn. Soon it becomes clear that they have a powerful connection rooted in the past…but can any vow stand the test of time?

* * * *

Hades: A Demonica Underworld Novella

by Larissa Ione

A fallen angel with a mean streak and a mohawk, Hades has spent thousands of years serving as Jailor of the Underworld. The souls he guards are as evil as they come, but few dare to cross him. All of that changes when a sexy fallen angel infiltrates his prison and unintentionally starts a riot. It's easy enough to quell an uprising, but for the first time, Hades is torn between delivering justice — or bestowing mercy — on the beautiful female who could be his salvation...or his undoing.

Thanks to her unwitting participation in another angel's plot to start Armageddon, Cataclysm was kicked out of Heaven and is now a fallen angel in service of Hades's boss, Azagoth. All she wants is to redeem herself and get back where she belongs. But when she gets trapped in Hades's prison domain with only the cocky but irresistible Hades to help her, Cat finds that where she belongs might be in the place she least expected...

* * * *

Azagoth: A Demonica Underword Novella

by Larissa Ione

Even in the fathomless depths of the underworld and the bleak chambers of a damaged heart, the bonds of love can heal...or destroy.

He holds the ability to annihilate souls in the palm of his hand. He commands the respect of the most dangerous of demons and the most powerful of angels. He can seduce and dominate any female he wants with a mere look. But for all Azagoth's power, he's bound by shackles of his own making, and only an angel with a secret holds the key to his release.

She's an angel with the extraordinary ability to travel through time and space. An angel with a tormented past she can't escape. And when Lilliana is sent to Azagoth's underworld realm, she finds that her past isn't all she can't escape. For the irresistibly sexy fallen angel known as Azagoth is also known as the Grim Reaper, and when he claims a soul, it's forever...

Reaper: A Demonica Novel

By Larissa Ione

Now available.

THE DEMONICA SERIES RETURNS...

He is the Keeper of Souls. Judge, jury, and executioner. He is death personified.

He is the Grim Reaper.

A fallen angel who commands the respect of both Heaven and Hell, Azagoth has presided over his own underworld realm for thousands of years. As the overlord of evil souls, he maintains balance crucial to the existence of life on Earth and beyond. But as all the realms gear up for the prophesied End of Days, the ties that bind him to Sheoul-gra have begun to chafe.

Now, with his beloved mate and unborn child the target of an ancient enemy, Azagoth will stop at nothing to save them, even if it means breaking blood oaths and shattering age-old alliances.

Even if it means destroying himself and setting the world on fire…

* * * *

Lilliana woke to someone tap dancing on her bladder.

Groaning, she rolled over and bumped into Azagoth. Pleasantly surprised that he was still in bed, she ignored her need to pee and curled up against him.

She'd missed this so much while she was gone.

"Good morning," he murmured, his husky voice even more gravelly than usual.

"Morning." She snuggled into his shoulder. "I'm surprised you're not working."

He yawned. "You wore me out last night."

Smiling against his skin, she trailed her fingers along the hard ridges and deep valleys of his abs.

"I wanted to show you how grateful I was that you threw me a baby shower." And she'd done it without getting *too* active. Eidolon couldn't begrudge her *one* orgasm, right?

"Mmm." He pressed a kiss into her hair. "You must have been *very* grateful."

She slid her hand under the sheet and meandered her way to the curve of his hip. She might be a million months into her pregnancy, but her sex drive didn't care in the least.

"I'm still grateful."

He hissed as her knuckles brushed his shaft. "Not complaining."

It truly had been sweet of him to gather together the denizens of Sheoul-gra for a big celebration of food, drink, and games in the traditions of people from the human, demon, and angelic cultures. She'd suffered two more bouts of intense nausea and some cramps, but they'd passed quickly. What hadn't passed was Azagoth's concern.

Which was probably why he was still in bed with her.

It was cute the way he hovered. Annoying at times, but cute.

"I just want you to know that you're my life," he said. "Without you, I'm a monster."

"And what are you *with* me?"

He gave her a rare, boyish grin, made even more playful by his mop of bedhead. "A *happy* monster."

"I'm very happy about the happy." She rubbed her eyes and yawned.

"Things are good, Lil," he said. "I never thought much about being a partner, let alone a parent, but I want to do these things with you." He settled his hand on her belly and smiled with wonder. "This will be my first child born without a predetermined future. He or she can be anything. Do anything."

"Incredible, isn't it?" She pushed up on one elbow and leaned in to kiss his chest. She'd kissed every inch of him last night. Maybe she'd lick every inch of him this morning. "And our baby will be born to parents who love each other."

Determined to show him how much she loved him, she kissed her way lower. Her lips whispered over his nipple, but before she could taste him, a cramp wrenched her insides. She sucked in a harsh breath, her hand going to her belly.

"What is it?" Azagoth jackknifed up, his expression dark with worry. "Is it the baby?"

Fierce heat swelled beneath the surface of her skin as her abdomen tightened. "I think it might be Braxton Hicks," she said between panting breaths.

"What?"

"Cara had them." Closing her eyes to stop the room from spinning, she eased back onto her pillow. "They're like practice contractions."

She didn't remember Cara complaining about being hot and sweating buckets, though. Another cramp streaked through her, and she moaned. Cara *had* said they were painful, as if someone were squeezing her intestines.

This was more like someone was driving a red-hot blade through them.

"You're white as a ghost, Lilli."

Something's wrong.

No, nothing was wrong. She was being paranoid.

Azagoth rested his palm on her forehead, testing her temperature. "Are these Hicks things supposed to be like this?"

She heard the panic in his voice but not the words. Her ears were buzzing. Her head was pounding. And, suddenly, a wave of agony wrapped around her and squeezed so hard she screamed. Vaguely, she heard Azagoth call out her name as a warm gush spread between her thighs.

"Lilliana? Lilliana!" His voice droned in and out as the room began to tilt. There was shouting. More pain. Her thoughts fragmented.

And then, finally…nothing.

About Larissa Ione

Air Force veteran Larissa Ione traded in a career as a meteorologist to pursue her passion of writing. She has since published dozens of books, hit several bestseller lists, including the New York Times and USA Today, and has been nominated for a RITA award. She now spends her days in pajamas with her computer, strong coffee, and fictional worlds. She believes in celebrating everything, and would never be caught without a bottle of Champagne chilling in the fridge…just in case. After a dozen moves all over the country with her now-retired U.S. Coast Guard spouse, she is now settled in Wisconsin with her husband, her teenage son, a rescue cat named Vegas, and her very own hellhounds, a King Shepherd named Hexe, and a Belgian Malinois named Duvel.

For more information about Larissa, visit www.larissaione.com.

Discover 1001 Dark Nights

COLLECTION ONE
FOREVER WICKED by Shayla Black ~ CRIMSON TWILIGHT by Heather Graham ~ CAPTURED IN SURRENDER by Liliana Hart ~ SILENT BITE: A SCANGUARDS WEDDING by Tina Folsom ~ DUNGEON GAMES by Lexi Blake ~ AZAGOTH by Larissa Ione ~ NEED YOU NOW by Lisa Renee Jones ~ SHOW ME, BABY by Cherise Sinclair~ ROPED IN by Lorelei James ~ TEMPTED BY MIDNIGHT by Lara Adrian ~ THE FLAME by Christopher Rice ~ CARESS OF DARKNESS by Julie Kenner

COLLECTION TWO
WICKED WOLF by Carrie Ann Ryan ~ WHEN IRISH EYES ARE HAUNTING by Heather Graham ~ EASY WITH YOU by Kristen Proby ~ MASTER OF FREEDOM by Cherise Sinclair ~ CARESS OF PLEASURE by Julie Kenner ~ ADORED by Lexi Blake ~ HADES by Larissa Ione ~ RAVAGED by Elisabeth Naughton ~ DREAM OF YOU by Jennifer L. Armentrout ~ STRIPPED DOWN by Lorelei James ~ RAGE/KILLIAN by Alexandra Ivy/Laura Wright ~ DRAGON KING by Donna Grant ~ PURE WICKED by Shayla Black ~ HARD AS STEEL by Laura Kaye ~ STROKE OF MIDNIGHT by Lara Adrian ~ ALL HALLOWS EVE by Heather Graham ~ KISS THE FLAME by Christopher Rice~ DARING HER LOVE by Melissa Foster ~ TEASED by Rebecca Zanetti ~ THE PROMISE OF SURRENDER by Liliana Hart

COLLECTION THREE
HIDDEN INK by Carrie Ann Ryan ~ BLOOD ON THE BAYOU by Heather Graham ~ SEARCHING FOR MINE by Jennifer Probst ~ DANCE OF DESIRE by Christopher Rice ~ ROUGH RHYTHM by Tessa Bailey ~ DEVOTED by Lexi Blake ~ Z by Larissa Ione ~ FALLING UNDER YOU by Laurelin Paige ~ EASY FOR KEEPS by Kristen Proby ~ UNCHAINED by Elisabeth Naughton ~ HARD TO SERVE by Laura Kaye ~ DRAGON FEVER by Donna Grant ~ KAYDEN/SIMON by Alexandra Ivy/Laura Wright ~ STRUNG UP by Lorelei James ~ MIDNIGHT UNTAMED by Lara Adrian ~ TRICKED by Rebecca Zanetti ~ DIRTY WICKED by Shayla Black ~

THE ONLY ONE by Lauren Blakely ~ SWEET SURRENDER by Liliana Hart

COLLECTION FOUR

ROCK CHICK REAWAKENING by Kristen Ashley ~ ADORING INK by Carrie Ann Ryan ~ SWEET RIVALRY by K. Bromberg ~ SHADE'S LADY by Joanna Wylde ~ RAZR by Larissa Ione ~ ARRANGED by Lexi Blake ~ TANGLED by Rebecca Zanetti ~ HOLD ME by J. Kenner ~ SOMEHOW, SOME WAY by Jennifer Probst ~ TOO CLOSE TO CALL by Tessa Bailey ~ HUNTED by Elisabeth Naughton ~ EYES ON YOU by Laura Kaye ~ BLADE by Alexandra Ivy/Laura Wright ~ DRAGON BURN by Donna Grant ~ TRIPPED OUT by Lorelei James ~ STUD FINDER by Lauren Blakely ~ MIDNIGHT UNLEASHED by Lara Adrian ~ HALLOW BE THE HAUNT by Heather Graham ~ DIRTY FILTHY FIX by Laurelin Paige ~ THE BED MATE by Kendall Ryan ~ NIGHT GAMES by CD Reiss ~ NO RESERVATIONS by Kristen Proby ~ DAWN OF SURRENDER by Liliana Hart

COLLECTION FIVE

BLAZE ERUPTING by Rebecca Zanetti ~ ROUGH RIDE by Kristen Ashley ~ HAWKYN by Larissa Ione ~ RIDE DIRTY by Laura Kaye ~ ROME'S CHANCE by Joanna Wylde ~ THE MARRIAGE ARRANGEMENT by Jennifer Probst ~ SURRENDER by Elisabeth Naughton ~ INKED NIGHTS by Carrie Ann Ryan ~ ENVY by Rachel Van Dyken ~ PROTECTED by Lexi Blake ~ THE PRINCE by Jennifer L. Armentrout ~ PLEASE ME by J. Kenner ~ WOUND TIGHT by Lorelei James ~ STRONG by Kylie Scott ~ DRAGON NIGHT by Donna Grant ~ TEMPTING BROOKE by Kristen Proby ~ HAUNTED BE THE HOLIDAYS by Heather Graham ~ CONTROL by K. Bromberg ~ HUNKY HEARTBREAKER by Kendall Ryan ~ THE DARKEST CAPTIVE by Gena Showalter

COLLECTION SIX

DRAGON CLAIMED by Donna Grant ~ ASHES TO INK by Carrie Ann Ryan ~ ENSNARED by Elisabeth Naughton ~ EVERMORE by Corinne Michaels ~ VENGEANCE by Rebecca Zanetti ~ ELI'S TRIUMPH by Joanna Wylde ~ CIPHER by Larissa Ione ~ RESCUING MACIE by Susan Stoker ~ ENCHANTED by Lexi Blake

~ TAKE THE BRIDE by Carly Phillips ~ INDULGE ME by J. Kenner ~ THE KING by Jennifer L. Armentrout ~ QUIET MAN by Kristen Ashley ~ ABANDON by Rachel Van Dyken ~ THE OPEN DOOR by Laurelin Paige ~ CLOSER by Kylie Scott ~ SOMETHING JUST LIKE THIS by Jennifer Probst ~ BLOOD NIGHT by Heather Graham ~ TWIST OF FATE by Jill Shalvis ~ MORE THAN PLEASURE YOU by Shayla Black ~ WONDER WITH ME by Kristen Proby ~ THE DARKEST ASSASSIN by Gena Showalter

COLLECTION SEVEN

THE BISHOP by Skye Warren ~ TAKEN WITH YOU by Carrie Ann Ryan ~ DRAGON LOST by Donna Grant ~ SEXY LOVE by Carly Phillips ~ PROVOKE by Rachel Van Dyken ~ RAFE by Sawyer Bennett ~ THE NAUGHTY PRINCESS by Claire Contreras ~ THE GRAVEYARD SHIFT by Darynda Jones ~ CHARMED by Lexi Blake ~ SACRIFICE OF DARKNESS by Alexandra Ivy ~ THE QUEEN by Jen Armentrout ~ BEGIN AGAIN by Jennifer Probst ~ VIXEN by Rebecca Zanetti ~ SLASH by Laurelin Paige ~ THE DEAD HEAT OF SUMMER by Heather Graham ~ WILD FIRE by Kristen Ashley ~ MORE THAN PROTECT YOU by Shayla Black ~ LOVE SONG by Kylie Scott ~ CHERISH ME by J. Kenner ~ SHINE WITH ME by Kristen Proby

Discover Blue Box Press

TAME ME by J. Kenner ~ TEMPT ME by J. Kenner ~ DAMIEN by J. Kenner ~ TEASE ME by J. Kenner ~ REAPER by Larissa Ione ~ THE SURRENDER GATE by Christopher Rice ~ SERVICING THE TARGET by Cherise Sinclair ~ THE LAKE OF LEARNING by Steve Berry and M.J. Rose ~ THE MUSEUM OF MYSTERIES by Steve Berry and M.J. Rose ~ TEASE ME by J. Kenner ~ FROM BLOOD AND ASH by Jennifer L. Armentrout ~ QUEEN MOVE by Kennedy Ryan ~ THE HOUSE OF LONG AGO by Steve Berry and M.J. Rose ~ THE BUTTERFLY ROOM by Lucinda Riley ~ A KINGDOM OF FLESH AND FIRE by Jennifer L. Armentrout

On Behalf of 1001 Dark Nights,

Liz Berry, M.J. Rose, and Jillian Stein would like to thank ~

Steve Berry
Doug Scofield
Benjamin Stein
Kim Guidroz
Social Butterfly PR
Ashley Wells
Asha Hossain
Chris Graham
Chelle Olson
Kasi Alexander
Jessica Johns
Dylan Stockton
Richard Blake
and Simon Lipskar